MY FAVOURITE
MOUNTAINEERING
STORIES

In the same series

MY FAVOURITE MUSIC STORIES
edited by Yehudi Menuhin

MY FAVOURITE ESCAPE STORIES
edited by Pat Reid

MY FAVOURITE CRICKET STORIES
edited by John Arlott

MY FAVOURITE ANIMAL STORIES
edited by Gerald Durrell

MY FAVOURITE DOG STORIES
edited by Douglas Bader

MY FAVOURITE HORSE STORIES
edited by Dorian Williams

MY FAVOURITE STORIES OF IRELAND
edited by Bríd Mahon

MY FAVOURITE STORIES OF SCOTLAND
edited by John Laurie

and other titles

My Favourite MOUNTAINEERING STORIES

edited by
JOHN HUNT

with line decorations by
DOUGLAS PHILLIPS

LUTTERWORTH PRESS
GUILDFORD AND LONDON

First published in this collected form 1978
Introduction and editorial links copyright © 1978 by
John Hunt (Lord Hunt of Llanfair Waterdine)

ISBN 0 7188 2375 3

EDITORIAL NOTE

Metric equivalents for measurements of the heights of
mountains and of the distances of particular stages of
climbs have been added in square brackets following
Imperial references. No equivalent, however, has been
added for such general phrases as 'several miles' or
'a few feet'. When a particular Imperial measurement is
referred to several times in a single passage, the Metric
equivalent is given after the first reference only.

Set in 12 point Bembo

Printed in Great Britain by
Ebenezer Baylis & Son Limited
The Trinity Press, Worcester, and London

Contents

CONTENTS

Acknowledgments

The editor and the publishers are indebted to all those who have given permission for the use of copyright material, or who have helped in the obtaining of that permission:

William Heinemann Ltd, for 'Trams and Trains' from *Climbing The Fish's Tail* and 'Walking to Everest' from *South Col*, both by Wilfrid Noyce

Mr and Mrs R. Scott Russell, executors of the Estate of the late George Ingle Finch, for 'Early Days' from *The Making Of A Mountaineer*, by George Ingle Finch

Methuen & Co. Ltd, for 'A Memory of the Mischabel' from *On High Hills*, by Geoffrey Winthrop Young

Hodder & Stoughton Ltd, for 'Nanda Devi' from *Upon That Mountain*, by Eric Shipton

J. M. Dent & Sons Ltd, for 'Via Della Pera' from *Brenva*, by T. Graham Brown

William Blackwood & Sons Ltd, and the Estate of the late F. S. Smythe, for 'The West Buttress of Clogwyn du'r Arddu' from *Climbs And Ski Runs* by F. S. Smythe

Hodder & Stoughton Ltd, for 'Head-First to Life' from *Nanga Parbat Pilgrimage*, by Hermann Buhl

Curtis Brown Ltd, for 'Up the Ridge and Down a Crevasse' from *The Red Snows*, by Christopher Brasher and Sir John Hunt, published by the Hutchinson Publishing Group

Hodder & Stoughton Ltd, for 'The Summit: 1953', written by Edmund Hillary and taken from *The Ascent Of Everest* by Sir John Hunt

Hodder & Stoughton Ltd, for 'The Summit: 1975', written by Dougal Haston and Doug Scott, and taken from *Everest The Hard Way*, by Chris Bonington

'The First Ascent of the Matterhorn', from *Scrambles Amongst The Alps* by Edward Whymper, is quoted with the permission of the publishers from the text published by John Murray (Publishers) Ltd.

Introduction

The stories contained in this book are about relationships between men and mountains, and between people engaged in climbing mountains. Mountains cast a spell on many people and, for some of us, there is a deep-seated urge to respond to their challenge. Human beings have begun to experience this curious compulsion in fairly recent times; with few exceptions, references to the mountain scenes were, before the last century, coloured by the sense of awe, or fear, in which the great peaks were held in the minds of our ancestors. Those remote and apparently impregnable fastnesses were once held to be the abode of the gods and, later, of dragons. It is only just over a hundred years ago that some educated travellers in Europe, with British citizens in the van, thought to venture towards the distant summits, hiring the experience of mountain peasants in finding their way. Mountaineering, first in an exploratory and later in a sporting sense, which made its debut in the Western Alps in the first half of the nineteenth century, developed apace; within fifty years nearly all the alpine peaks had been climbed. The new breed of mountaineers had greatly increased, though still only among the relatively wealthy classes. Some were already active in more remote and higher ranges, others were attempting harder ways to the summits of peaks which had already been climbed, or were developing the skills of rock-climbing on crags and cliffs in their own homelands. Indeed, the daring notion of attempting Everest, which had been established in 1852 as the highest point on the Earth's surface, was suggested in 1883 to a future President of the Royal Geographical Society by a future leader of two early expeditions to that mountain, which took place shortly after the First World War. Today, the progress recorded in the Alps before 1900 is being repeated in the Himalayas and other high ranges all over the globe; as a sport, it attracts large numbers of men and women irrespective of social status.

I have chosen the stories which follow partly because they illustrate this progress in mountain climbing over the past hundred years; partly because they give some insight into the contrasting or complementary attractions which draw men and women to the heights; most of all because each story has had a special appeal to myself over the years since I started to climb. With the exception of Whymper with whom, so my mother told me, my father once climbed, I have known all the authors personally and have climbed with several of them. Some of the experiences which they relate are similar to my own; a few of them have been shared with the writers. My copy of *The Making of a Mountaineer* has on its fly sheet the words 'Xmas 1924 from Granny'. I was then fourteen and it was George Finch's book, together with the news that summer from one of those early Everest Expeditions that Mallory and Irvine had died near the summit, which made me decide to become a mountaineer myself. This is why I have chosen that author's personal account of his own beginnings as the first chapter.

Mountaineering is a sport inseparable from danger. Without the possibility of serious accidents it would lose a great part of its appeal. For this reason I have included one story which ended in tragedy. Three of the authors I have selected, and a number of the people they mention, were later killed in the mountains. I hope that readers may discern through these stories an element in mountaineering which transcends the limits of sport as it is popularly understood. It is almost as though man is intent on perpetuating the struggle against the forces of nature because, or despite the fact that, he has so largely succeeded in harnessing them. That continuing compulsion may be glimpsed in the poem *Walking to Everest* by Wilfrid Noyce, which he wrote during our halts for meals and rest during the long trail to Everest in 1953. Eric Shipton, in his description of his party's pioneering journey through the gorge of the Rishi Ganga to reach the sanctuary of Nanda Devi, reveals another relationship between men and mountains in which the mountain lover seeks, albeit by way of effort and privation, not war but peace with his rugged environment. Whatever it is that draws us to the peaks the goal of our endeavours is, for many, less of a sport, more a way of life. And like life, mountaineering contains a great deal of fun.

John Hunt.

To
WILFRID NOYCE
1917–1962

Prologue

Away, good God! with trams and trains
and standing in the endless queue
and catching buses when it rains
and work, and chores I *have* to do.
Away with my employer's eye
and office tea, unmixed with love,
and typing trash, and wondering why,
and clocks with hands that will not move.
Away with prams, say I, that we
must push because the neighbours do
by railed-in park and cemetery,
on paths so neat, past flowers so few.
Let me not eat from tins, great God,
but feed upon an air that's clean;
up valleys that no foot has trod
see snows till now by man unseen.

Let me go climb those virgin snows,
leave the dark stain of man behind.
Let me adventure—and heaven knows
grateful shall be my quiet mind.

Now I'm alone, and I'm afraid.
The wind is cold, the stars are high.
Coffee and cake were surely made
to ease a mountain's cruelty.

The ice peak is before me still,
a ghost white-masked, a monster form;
weakly my heart bends to my will,
my chilled hands cringe in the glove to warm.
Mist creeps from the valley floor
and camp's a hundred miles away.
A flake falls, two snowflakes more,
the air is dyed to dunnest grey.
My comrade's turned, and I'm alone.
Great God! for all the homely things,
for Primrose Villa, for the one
answer to foolish questionings!
For gas, for baths, for buttered toast,
for cosy buses when it rains,
for Lyons' lunch, for work the most—
Praise be to God for trams and trains!

taken from
CLIMBING THE FISH'S TAIL
by Wilfrid Noyce.
see also page 109

I

Early Days

GEORGE FINCH

George Finch, a distinguished physicist, came to prominence as a climber in the years preceding the First World War. At a time when it was considered to be almost axiomatic that the services of qualified professional guides should be engaged for this dangerous activity, George with his brother Max and a few kindred spirits was already setting the vogue for guideless climbing, which is now almost universal, producing the highest standards of skill and experience among those who climb only as a leisure pastime. George Finch was a predictable choice for the early Everest expeditions. His professional knowledge played an important part in developing the use of oxygen at high altitudes at a time when prevailing mountaineering opinion strongly opposed it.

Some twenty-two years ago, on a dewy spring morning in October, I urged my panting pony towards a hill-top in the Australian bush, the better to spy out the whereabouts of a mob of wallaby. The last few feet of the ascent being too much for the pony, I dismounted and, leaving him behind, scrambled up a short, rocky chimney to the summit. The wallaby were nowhere to be seen; but my wondering eyes were held spellbound by such a vision as I had never even dreamed of. Miles and miles away the white-washed roofs of the township of Orange gleamed brightly in the clear morning sunshine; the main roads converging upon the town showed sharp and distinct from out their setting in the rolling bush. The picture was beautiful: precise and accurate as the work of a draughtsman's pen, but fuller of meaning than any map. I was just thirteen years old, and for the first time in my life the true significance of geography began to dawn upon me; and with the dawning was born a resolution that was to colour and widen my whole life. Before returning to my pony after this, my first mountain ascent, I had made up my mind to see the world; to see it from above, from the tops of mountains, whence I could get that wide and comprehensive view which is denied to those who observe things from their own plane.

A year later my brother Maxwell and I, now proud possessors of Edward Whymper's *Scrambles Amongst the Alps*, emulated our hero's early exploits by scaling Beachy Head by a particularly dangerous route, much to the consternation of the lighthouse crew and subsequent disappointment of the coastguards who arrived up aloft with ropes and rescue tackle just in time to see us draw ourselves, muddy and begrimed, over the brink of the cliff into safety. That climb taught us many things; amongst them, that a cliff is often more difficult to climb than would appear from below; that flints embedded in chalk are not reliable hand-holds, but sometimes break away when one trusts one's weight to them; that there are people who delight in rolling stones down a cliff without troubling to see whether anyone is underneath; and that if it be good to look down upon the world, the vision is beautiful in proportion to the difficulties overcome in gaining the eminence. A few weeks later, an ascent of Notre-Dame by an unorthodox route might well have led to trouble, had it not been for the fact that the two gendarmes and the kindly priest who were the most interested spectators of these doings did not lack a sense of humour and human understanding. Then we passed through Basle into Switzerland, bitterly disappointed to find that the railway did not wind through dark, tortuous valleys bordered by glistening snow-capped mountains.

That winter we broke bounds. Shod in the lightest of shoes, with clothing ill-suited to protect against wind, with walking sticks, and a pocketful of sandwiches we took the train to Wesen. There we bought a map and set off to climb the Speer, a mountain barely 6,000 feet in height [1,830 metres], but nevertheless a formidable enough proposition for such an ill-equipped party in winter. All that day we struggled on, often knee-deep in snow. At dusk, still far from our goal, we sought refuge from the cold breezes of eventide. Letting ourselves in through the chimney hole in the roof of a snowed-up Alp hut, we bivouacked for the night. Shivering and sleepless we lay, watching the stars as they twinkled derisively in frosty clearness through the hole in the roof. After what seemed an eternity, morning came, and we plodded on with stiff and weary limbs to the summit. There, bathed in the warm sunshine, all hardships were forgotten, and we gazed longingly over to the ranges of the Tödi and the Glärnisch—real snow and ice mountains with great glaciers streaming down from their lofty crests. Thence the eye travelled away to the rich plains, the gleaming lakes and dark, forested hills of the lowlands, until details faded in the bluish mist of distance. Switzerland, a whole country, was at our feet. This escapade taught us further lessons: that mountaineering is a hungry game; that boots should be waterproof, and soles thick and studded with nails; that a thick warm coat can be an almost priceless possession.

Then came a glorious summer vacation of fishing and sailing round the coast of Majorca, with hours of splendid clambering on the cliffs of Miramar, followed by a week with our tutor on the Pilatus. Our tutor was a sportsman, and we scrambled about together to our hearts' content, more than once sailing as close to the wind as any of us have ever done since. And yet again we had learned something: that the stockinged foot finds a firmer hold on dry limestone than a nailed boot; that wet limestone slabs are slippery and an abomination to be avoided; that the thrusting muscles of one's legs are more powerful and more enduring than the pulling muscles of one's arms; and that strong fingers are of more use in climbing than a pair of well-developed biceps.

More holidays came and went: summers passed on the shores of the western Mediterranean, but Christmas vacations spent in Grindelwald, and devoted to learning the art of ski-ing. In Grindelwald we had the good fortune to win the liking of old Christian Jossi, in his day one of the greatest guides and best step-cutters in the Alps. He took us to the upper Grindelwald Glacier and on its mighty ice pinnacles, or séracs, taught us the elements of step-cutting in ice and the use of the rope. He showed us how to fashion a stairway in hard, blue ice, the floor of each step sloping inwards so that it was easy for one to stand securely. He showed us the points by which to judge of the merits of a good axe, how to hold and use it, and how, imitating him, to cut good safe steps with a minimum number of blows and expenditure of labour. He showed us how easy it is to check a slip and hold up a man on the rope provided it be kept always taut from man to man; and he did not hesitate to rub in, by demonstrations accompanied by much forceful language, what a fearful snare the rope could be if it were improperly used and permitted to be trailed loose and in coils between the various members of a party. He also pointed out some of the many varieties of snow: some good, in which on even the steepest slopes a kick or two sufficed to make a reliable step; others which could not be trusted on any but the gentlest of slopes and needing only a touch to start slithering down with an insidious hissing sound to form an avalanche which would sweep everything with it in its path of destruction. Last but not least, Christian Jossi instilled into us some of his own fervid love of the mountains and of mountain adventure.

The summer holidays of 1906 drew nigh. Our longing for mountain adventure was no longer to be denied, and elders and betters had perforce to give way. But they enforced two provisos —we were to be accompanied by guides, and climbing was to be restricted to the lesser Alps of Northern Switzerland. We climbed a few lesser summits, all about 10,000 feet high [3,050 metres]; on none was there climbing where hands as well as feet were required, and not once did we see the axe used to cut a step. Efforts to wheedle our stalwart guardians into attacking the bold pyramid of the Segnes Tschingelhorn, always provocatively before our eyes, failed miserably; they had their instructions. But they could not always keep us in sight, and more than once, stealing forth alone, we found good climbing, adventure and untrammelled fun; and the desire to climb without guides was born in us.

That winter the lesser peaks and passes of Grindelwald were visited on skis. A stern effort to gain the Strahlegg Pass was frustrated by a snowstorm in the teeth of which for nineteen hours on end we fought our way back to Grindelwald, having learnt that, with map and compass and given your bearings, bad weather in the mountains can be faced and even enjoyed if you only keep on moving and do not get flurried. We also knew now that boots should be large enough to enable two pairs of woollen socks to be worn without pinching the foot, and that toe-caps should be high and roomy so as not to interfere with the circulation. A sweater worn underneath a wind-proof jacket of sailcloth was found to be both lighter and much warmer than heavy tweeds through which the wind could blow and to which the snow would stick.

From 1907 onwards until 1911, Max and I both studied in Zürich and were thus thrown into close and continual contact with the mountains, from which we were separated only by some three or four hours by rail. Barely a week-end went by without our taking train to the mountains and climbing. During the Easter holidays of 1907 we betook ourselves on skis up to the Clariden hut, one of the many little shelters built by the Swiss Alpine Club in the heart of the mountains. These huts are furnished with straw-filled sleeping bunks, blankets, a small cooking stove, a supply of wood, and cooking and eating utensils. We had with us provisions for a week, during the whole of which period the weather was fine and snow conditions at their best. We climbed almost all the surrounding summits, the return to the hut each evening taking the form of an effortless run on skis over the Clariden Glacier.

During the summer vacation of the same year Max and I successfully obtained *carte blanche* to climb without guides, and for nearly three months we roamed in and about the range of the Tödi. We climbed most of the summits in the range, including the Tödi itself, which with its 11,800 feet [3,600 metres] of altitude was much the highest mountain so far grappled with. We always endeavoured to exercise every possible attention to the following out of the lessons hitherto learnt, losing no opportunity of acquiring fresh knowledge regarding matters of equipment, the handling of rope and axe, and the mountains themselves. In particular we aimed at cultivating a sense of route-finding and teaching ourselves how to use the map. The winter of that year saw us embarking upon expeditions of a more ambitious nature than those previously attempted. Up to the Easter of 1908 our most successful winter feat was an ascent of the Sustenhorn on skis; but during that vacation we accomplished the ascent of the Tödi, a winter expedition that even today is reckoned by no means a simple undertaking. As the summer holidays approached, a still more ambitious programme was drawn up. Our self-assurance, confidence—call it what you like—seems to have been boundless, for we now considered that our apprenticeship had been sufficiently long to justify us in letting ambitions soar into reality. The programme, although not carried out in its entirety, nevertheless proved a great success. Beginning with the Bernese Oberland, we climbed the Wetterhorn, were driven back by storm just below the summit of the Eiger, but followed up the reverse by climbing the Mönch, Jungfrau and Finsteraarhorn. Thence making our way down the Aletsch Glacier to the Rhône Valley, we went up to Zermatt. From there we climbed the Matterhorn and the Dent Blanche, then crossed over the Col d'Hérens to Arolla, where for the first time we experienced to the full the pleasures of traversing a mountain, that is, ascending by one route and descending by another. Amongst others, were traversed the Aiguille de la Za, the Aiguilles Rouges d'Arolla and the Pigne d'Arolla. The ascent of the last-named was made by cutting steps up the steep north face, and it was this climb more than any other that won me over to the delights of ice-climbing. Returning to Zermatt by various high-level passes, we journeyed northwards and wound up the season in the Tödi district, where all the major summits were traversed.

Thus from its chance nucleus on the hill-top in the Australian bush, snowball-wise the zest for the mountains grew until it has actually become an integral part of life itself. The health and happiness that the passion has brought with it are as incalculable as the ways of the 'divinity that shapes our ends', chooses our parents for us, and places us in a certain environment. The love that Max and I have for the mountains I cannot but attribute to the fact that we were possessed of a father who taught us from our earliest years to love the open spaces of the earth, encouraged us to seek adventure and provided the wherewithal for us to enjoy the quest and, above all, looked to us to fight our own battles and rely on our own resources.

2

The First Ascent Of The Matterhorn

EDWARD WHYMPER

It is not surprising that George Finch referred to Whymper's Scrambles Amongst The Alps *as having been an inspiration for his own beginnings as a mountaineer, for it was Whymper and his contemporaries who were the pioneers of this adventurous pastime. The first ascent of the Matterhorn was almost as much the focus of public attention and acclaim as was that of Everest nearly a century later. By many people it was adjudged impossible to scale this fantastic fang, so familiar today to tourists, and others who have never seen it with the naked eye, from all over the world. When Whymper and his companions assembled at the foot of its North-East, or Swiss, ridge in July 1865, no less than fourteen previous attempts had been made, mostly from the opposite, Italian side. Nearly all the amateurs concerned in these efforts to solve the problem were from Britain, usually with Italian guides, occasionally alone. One of those guides, the Italian Jean-Antoine Carrel, had conceived a very personal ambition to be the first to reach the summit. It is against this background that the triumph of Whymper's party, which included a brilliant French guide and two local Swiss from Zermatt, should be read.*

We started from Zermatt on the 13th of July 1865 at half-past five, on a brilliant and perfectly cloudless morning. We were eight in number—Croz, old Peter and his two sons, Lord F. Douglas, Hadow, Hudson, and I. To ensure steady motion, one tourist and one native walked together. The youngest

Taugwalder fell to my share, and the lad marched well, proud to be on the expedition, and happy to show his powers. The wine-bags also fell to my lot to carry, and throughout the day, after each drink, I replenished them secretly with water, so that at the next halt they were found fuller than before! This was considered a good omen, and little short of miraculous.

On the first day we did not intend to ascend to any great height, and we mounted, accordingly, very leisurely; picked up the things which were left in the chapel at the Schwarzsee at 8.20, and proceeded thence along the ridge connecting the Hörnli with the Matterhorn. At half-past eleven we arrived at the base of the actual peak; then quitted the ridge, and clambered round some ledges on to the eastern face. We were now fairly upon the mountain, and were astonished to find that places which from the Riffel, or even from the Furggengletscher, looked entirely impracticable, were so easy that we could run about.

Before twelve o'clock we had found a good position for the tent, at a height of 11,000 feet [3,350 metres]. Croz and young Peter went on to see what was above, in order to save time on the following morning. They cut across the heads of the snow-slopes which descended towards the Furggengletscher, and disappeared round a corner; but shortly afterwards we saw them high up on the face, moving quickly. We others made a solid platform for the tent in a well-protected spot, and then watched eagerly for the return of the men. The stones which they upset told us that they were very high, and we proposed that the way must be easy. At length, just before 3 p.m., we saw them coming down, evidently much excited. 'What are they saying, Peter?' 'Gentlemen, they say it is no good.' But when they came near we heard a different story. 'Nothing but what was good; not a difficulty, not a single difficulty. We could have gone to the summit and returned today easily!'

We passed the remaining hours of daylight—some basking in the sunshine, some sketching or collecting; and when the sun went down, giving, as it departed, a glorious promise for the morrow, we returned to the tent to arrange for the night. Hudson made tea, I coffee, and we then retired each one to his blanket-bag—the Taugwalders, Lord Francis Douglas, and myself occupying the tent; the others remaining, by preference, outside. Long after dusk the cliffs above echoed with our laughter and with the songs of the guides; for we were happy that night in camp, and feared no evil.

We assembled together outside the tent before dawn on the morning of the 14th, and started directly it was light enough to move. Young Peter came on with us as a guide, and his brother returned to Zermatt. We followed the route which had been taken on the previous day, and in a few minutes turned the rib which had intercepted the view of the eastern face from our tent platform. The whole of this great slope was now revealed, rising for 3,000 feet [915 metres], like a huge natural staircase. Some parts were more and others were less easy; but we were not once brought to a halt by any serious impediment, for when an obstruction was met in front it could always be turned to the right or to the left. For the greater part of the way there was, indeed, no occasion for the rope and sometimes Hudson led, sometimes myself. At 6.20 we had attained a height of 12,800 feet [3,900 metres], and halted for half an hour; we then continued the ascent without a break until 9.55, when we stopped for fifty minutes, at a height of 14,000 feet [4,270 metres]. Twice we struck the N.E. ridge and followed it for some little distance—to no advantage, for it was usually more rotten and steep, and always more difficult than the face. Still, we kept near to it, lest stones perchance might fall.

We had now arrived at the foot of that part which, from the Riffelberg or from Zermatt, seems perpendicular or over-hanging, and could no longer continue upon the eastern side. For a little distance we ascended by snow upon the arête—that is, the ridge—descending towards Zermatt, and then, by common consent, turned over to the right, or to the northern side. Before doing so, we made a change in the order of ascent. Croz went first, I followed, Hudson came third; Hadow and old Peter were last. 'Now,' said Croz, as he led off—'now for something altogether different.' The work became difficult, and required caution. In some places there was little to hold, and it was desirable that those should be in front who were least likely to slip. The general slope of the mountain at this part was less than 40°, and snow had accumulated in, and had filled up, the interstices of the rock face, leaving only occasional fragments projecting here and there. These were at times covered with a thin film of ice, produced from the melting and refreezing of the snow. It was the counterpart, on a small scale, of the upper

700 feet [213 metres] of the Pointe des Ecrins; only there was this material difference—the face of the Ecrins was about, or exceeded, an angle of 50°, and the Matterhorn face was less than 40°. It was a place over which any fair mountaineer might pass in safety, and Mr Hudson ascended this part, and, as far as I know, the entire mountain, without having the slightest assistance rendered to him upon any occasion. Sometimes, after I had taken a hand from Croz, or received a pull, I turned to offer the same to Hudson; but he invariably declined, saying it was not necessary. Mr Hadow, however, was not accustomed to this kind of work, and required continual assistance. It is only fair to say that the difficulty which he found at this part arose simply and entirely from want of experience.

The solitary difficult part was of no great extent. We bore away over it at first, nearly horizontally, for a distance of about 400 feet [120 metres]; then ascended directly towards the summit for about 60 feet [18·25 metres]; then doubled back to the ridge which descends towards Zermatt. A long stride round a rather awkward corner brought us to snow once more. The last doubt vanished! The Matterhorn was ours! Nothing but 200 feet [61 metres] of easy snow remained to be surmounted!

You must now carry your thoughts back to the seven Italians who started from Breuil on the 11th of July. Four days had passed since their departure, and we were tormented with anxiety lest they should arrive on the top before us. All the way up we had talked of them, and many false alarms of 'men on the summit' had been raised. The higher we rose, the more intense became the excitement. What if we should be beaten at the last moment? The slope eased off, at length we could be detached, and Croz and I, dashing away, ran a neck-and-neck race, which ended in a dead heat. At 1.40 p.m. the world was at our feet, and the Matterhorn was conquered. Hurrah! Not a footstep could be seen.

It was not yet certain that we had not been beaten. The summit of the Matterhorn was formed of a rudely level ridge, about 350 feet long [107 metres] and the Italians might have been at its farther extremity. I hastened to the southern end, scanning the snow right and left eagerly. Hurrah again—it was untrodden! 'Where were the men?' I peered over the cliff, half doubting, half expectant, and saw them immediately—mere dots on the ridge, at an immense distance below. Up went my arms and my hat. 'Croz! Croz! come here!' 'Where are they, Monsieur?' 'There—don't you see them—down there!' 'Ah! the *coquins*, they are low down.' 'Croz, we must make those fellows hear us.' We yelled until we were hoarse. The Italians seemed to regard us—we could not be certain. 'Croz, we *must* make them hear us; they *shall* hear us!' I seized a block of rock and hurled it down, and called upon my companion, in the name of friendship, to do the same. We drove our sticks in, and prized away the crags, and soon a torrent of stones poured down the cliffs. There was no mistake about it this time. The Italians turned and fled.

Still, I would that the leader of that party could have stood with us at that moment, for our victorious shouts conveyed to him the disappointment of the ambition of a lifetime. He was the man, of all those who attempted the ascent of the Matterhorn, who most deserved to be the first upon its summit. He was the first to doubt its inaccessibility, and he was the only man who persisted in believing that its ascent would be accomplished. It was the aim of his life to make the ascent from the side of Italy, for the honour of his native valley. For a time he had the game in his hands: he played it as he thought best; but he made a false move, and he lost it.

The others had arrived, so we went back to the northern end of the ridge. Croz now took the tent-pole, and planted it in the highest snow. 'Yes,' we said, 'there is the flag-staff, but where is the flag?' 'Here it is,' he answered, pulling off his blouse and fixing it to the stick. It made a poor flag, and there was no wind to float it out, yet it was seen all round. They saw it at Zermatt— at the Riffel—in the Val Tournanche. At Breuil the watchers cried, 'Victory is ours!' They raised 'bravos' for Carrel and 'vivas' for Italy, and hastened to put themselves *en fête*. On the morrow they were undeceived. 'All was changed; the explorers returned sad—cast down—disheartened—confounded—gloomy.' 'It is true,' said the men. 'We saw them ourselves—they hurled stones at us! The old traditions *are* true—there are spirits on the top of the Matterhorn!'

We returned to the southern end of the ridge to build a cairn, and then paid homage to the view. The day was one of those superlatively calm and clear ones which usually precede bad weather. The atmosphere was perfectly still, and free from all clouds or vapours. Mountains fifty—nay a hundred—miles off, looked sharp and near. All their details—ridge and crag, snow and glacier—stood out with faultless definition. Pleasant thoughts of happy days in bygone years came up unbidden, as we recognized the old familiar forms. All were revealed—not one of the principal peaks of the Alps was hidden. I see them clearly now—the great inner circles of giants, backed by the ranges, chains, and massifs. There were forests black and gloomy, and meadows bright and lively; bounding water-falls and tranquil lakes; fertile lands and savage wastes; sunny plains and frigid plateaux. There were the most rugged forms, and the most graceful outlines—bold, perpendicular cliffs, and gentle, undulating slopes; rocky mountains and snowy mountains, sombre and solemn, or glittering and white, with walls—turrets—pinnacles—pyramids—domes—cones—and spires! These were every combination that the world can give, and every contrast that the heart could desire.

We remained on the summit for one hour—

'One crowded hour of glorious life.'

It passed away too quickly, and we began to prepare for the descent.

Hudson and I again consulted as to the best and safest arrangement of the party. We agreed that it would be best for Croz to go first, and Hadow second; Hudson, who was almost equal to a born mountaineer in sureness of foot, wished to be third; Lord Francis Douglas was placed next; and old Peter, the strongest of the remainder, after him. I suggested to Hudson that we should attach a rope to the rocks on our arrival at the difficult bit, and hold it as we descended, as an additional protection. He approved the idea, but it was not definitely settled that it should be done. The party was being arranged in the above order whilst I was sketching the summit, and they had finished, and were waiting for me to be tied in line, when someone remembered that our names had not been left in a bottle. They requested me to write them down, and moved off while it was being done.

A few minutes afterwards I tied myself to young Peter, ran down after the others, and caught them just as they were commencing the descent of the difficult part. Great care was being taken. Only one man was moving at a time; when he was firmly planted the next advanced, and so on. They had not, however, attached the additional rope to rocks, and nothing was said about it. The suggestion was not made for my own sake, and I am not sure that it even occurred to me again. For some little distance we two followed the others, detached from them, and should have continued so had not Lord Francis Douglas asked me, about 3 p.m., to tie on to old Peter, as he feared, he said, that Taugwalder would not be able to hold his ground if a slip occurred.

A few minutes later a sharp-eyed lad ran into the Monte Rosa hotel, to Seiler, saying that he had seen an avalanche fall from the summit of the Matterhorn on to the Matterhorn-gletscher. The boy was reproved for telling idle stories; he was right, nevertheless, and this was what he saw.

Michel Croz had laid aside his axe, and in order to give Mr Hadow greater security, was absolutely taking hold of his legs, and putting his feet, one by one, into their proper positions. So far as I know, no one was actually descending. I cannot speak with certainty, because the two leading men were partially hidden from my sight by an intervening mass of rock, but it is my belief, from the movements of their shoulders, that Croz, having done as I have said, was in the act of turning round, to go down a step or two himself; at this moment Mr Hadow slipped, fell against him, and knocked him over. I heard one startled exclamation from Croz, then saw him and Mr Hadow flying downwards; in another moment Hudson was dragged from his steps, and Lord F. Douglas immediately after him. All this was the work of a moment. Immediately we heard Croz's exclamation, old Peter and I planted ourselves as firmly as the rocks would permit: the rope was taut between us, and the jerk came on us both as one man. We held; but the rope broke midway between Taugwalder and Lord Francis Douglas. For a few seconds we saw our unfortunate companions sliding down-wards on their backs, and spreading out their hands, endeavouring to save themselves. They passed from our sight uninjured, disappeared one by one, and fell from precipice to precipice on to the Matterhorngletscher below, a distance of nearly 4,000 feet in height [1,220 metres]. From the moment the rope broke it was impossible to help them.

So perished our comrades!

A Memory Of The Mischabel

GEOFFREY WINTHROP YOUNG

Geoffrey Young is one of the great figures in the history of mountaineering whose hey-day, like that of Finch, was in the early part of this century. Unlike Finch, Young climbed with guides; it was the combination of amateurs daring to believe that the impossible-looking precipices of the Western Alps could be climbed, and the allied skill and strength of the leading professionals of those days, which raised the standards of mountaineering to new heights and lowered the credibility of that word 'impossible'. Geoffrey Young has been an inspiration to younger climbers, not only by the encouragement he gave them in his own time, but also through his ability to impart to later generations the spirit of mountaineering and the emotions of the climber, through his notable gifts as a writer.

The author is here describing how he and V. J. E. Ryan, with the guides Franz and Josef Lochmatter, and Josef Knubel, 'Little J.', made the first ascent of the South Face of the Täschhorn, near Zermatt.

The day was still bright and young, and the men obviously in fine climbing form. It was, therefore, no effort to telephone hearty remarks up and down the rope, or to emerge at Franz' feet after each struggle with a breathless but honest grin. But still the cliffs leaned out at us; still the unchancy upward and sideways traversing was forced upon us. A little cloud of anxiety crept upon the edge of my mind. My eye glanced unwillingly up or down: it was beginning to dodge, instinctively, the questions that the sight suggested. Our hands and feet grew gradually numb with the uninterrupted clinging to rounded, cold and slippery ledges.

At last—and how vividly the scene starts to mind—I stood on such a shelf, looking up at Franz' head and shoulders as he poised over a sheer wall above me, his prehensile feet balancing him erect upon a gutter-slope whose gracelessness I was yet to discover. The wall up to him bothered me a little, and as I got one arm over the coping and felt only the comfortless incline of the narrow band, I called out in joking patois, 'Watch out, Franz, for my rope!' He looked down at me and out beyond me thoughtfully, almost abstractedly, without the customary flash of big brown eyes and big white teeth: 'You must do what you can; here we can no longer help one another!' And then he turned away, dropping my rope symbolically from his hand and watching his brother, whose struggles, invisible to me, were audible far up round a black repulsive corner.

From such a man the words had the effect of an icy douche. The detachment of mind which a leader may never lose whatever his occupation with his own struggles returned upon the instant. I looked down over my arm: to see the deadly continuity of descending precipice with its narrow snowy eavelets leaning out one above another, and still one above another, dizzily; and seeming to shrug even the glance of my eye off into space. And I realized in a flash what a return down them must mean. I looked up: to discover that worse lay before us, if we failed to force a way up the chimney into which we were traversing for an escape. For hours already, deceived by our spacing from each other up a seeming ladder of terraces that were no terraces, we must have been climbing in reality at our several risks: each of us unprotected by the man above: the slip of any one imperilling the rest. For how many more hours would this, or could we, continue?

A slight, pricking snow began to drift across us. From the exposed height of our great pyramidal wall, surging above other ranges, we looked out across a frozen and unheeding stillness of white peak and glacier, disappearing under the darker clouds to the south. We seemed very much removed from the earth, and very much alone. As I turned back to the rock I could see nothing but antagonism in the ice-wrinkled face of the crags upon which we were venturing; and I had the feeling—it was too formless at the time to take the definite shape I must now give to it—as if somewhere low down beyond the horizon behind me a great grey bird was just lifting on its wings into heavy flight. As the hours wore on, this shadow at our backs seemed to be approaching soundlessly and covering more and more of the sky. Gradually it was enclosing us within its spread of cold wings, and isolating us from all the world of life and movement in our contest with the frigid wall of grey precipice.

Precariously we crawled up to and along, and up to and along, the sloping ribbons, silky with chill snow, and leading interruptedly upward towards the projecting corner which shut us off from the big couloir. On the decrepit mantelpiece by which we turned the corner itself, we could use a rock 'hitch' for the rope, one of the only three we found on all this upper face! We edged round into the couloir, a forbidding chasm; and found ourselves on a slim, shattered ledge, that continued inwards at a high level across the sheer wall of rock forming our side of the rift.

We were more or less together now; and no one could any longer pretend that some one above saw a gleam of hope denied to himself. Forty feet below [12 metres], the slabby back of the chasm slanted steeply outward, and down into space. Past us, the same backing of slabs mounted precipitously, to splay out in an amphitheatre of over-leaning walls far above. And every hopeless curve of slab was glassy with ice and glitter-film. The couloir, as an upward escape, needed no second glance. Josef was already clinging down our wall into the chasm below. His object was plain. The same belt or flaw by which we had entered the rift appeared again, at a lower level, upon the wall opposite to us, and disappeared round the profile of the further containing buttress. What could be seen of its re-start was no more than a sloping shelf, that wound steeply upwards and out of sight round the all but vertical corner. But Josef had evidently made up his mind that our only chance, now the couloir had failed, was to resume our perilous ribbon-traverses along the bands; in the hope—if they continued far enough—of finding the second, smaller chimney, the branch which forked out on to the south-east ridge, accessible; and if accessible, less icy-hearted. It appeared to me, and probably to him, a very faint and rather fearsome chance. Even the slabs below us, which gave difficult access to the crazy re-start of the traverse, looked villainous enough.

Josef moved tentatively about on the smooth shoot of the slabs, steadied by Ryan with the rope from our ledge. He never looked like crossing them; and I think that the nearer view of the re-start of the traverse was weakening his resolution. The dark chilly depths of the chasm gave muffled answer to his agitated comments. Franz, beside me on the ledge, watched him, hissing a gay little French song between his teeth, the only sign of excitement I have ever known him show. Then—'It won't go!' came in a hollow shout from below; and—'But it must go!' echoed from Franz, who at once leaped into action. I untied my rope to him. He was down and out on to the slabs in a breath, still singing to himself. He caterpillared his way across the ice-bosses above Josef. Josef, and other great guides, on slabs moved with the free poise of an athlete and the foot-cling of a chamois. Franz, in such case, had the habit and something of the appearance of a spider or crustacean. His curled head disappeared altogether. His body and square shoulders split and elongated into four steely tentacles, radiating from a small central core or hub of intelligence, which transmitted the messages between his tiny hands and boots as they clung attached and writhing at phenomenal angles and distances.

At the far side of the slabs he crawled on to and up the sloping shelf of the disappearing traverse, only keeping himself on it, so far as could be seen, by thrusting one foot firmly out against the aether. Presently Ryan followed, out of sight; and then Josef. Even with little J. playing my rope from high up on the wall behind me, I found the crossing of the iced slabs of the couloir upon a descending diagonal nasty enough. More especially towards the farther side, when the rope, sagging across from above, began to pull me back with a heavy draw. But the start of the traverse looked unspeakable. A downward and outward leaning shelf, with nothing below and an over-hanging wall above it, screwed steeply upward out of sight round the buttress. From far up along it came Josef's voice, thinly crying caution. How was I to keep on the shelf—and, much more, wriggle up it?

Little J. joined me on the ice-nicks in the slabs; and after many attempts the end of Josef's rope, slung from above and weighted with a stone, was lassoed back and round to a point on the slabs

3

from which we could recover it. I tied on, and started. Once up on the shelf, I found that there was nothing to keep me on it against the urgency of the slant into space. A hailing match between little J. and Josef only produced the information that while he was 'good' to hold—but not to pull—along the diagonal upward line of the shelf, he would be helpless against any direct downward strain, such as must result if I fell off the shelf. There was nothing for it but to thrust myself desperately upward, relying only upon the friction of my outer knee on the hem of the sloping ribbon to resist an outward drag to which the weight of the world seemed to be added. Of service, also, were two or three painful finger-tip pinches on the down-sloping prickles of the wall above my head.

When I reached Josef, I found him sprawled over rugosities on the buttress. His 'hitch'—the second of our dauntless three—was no more than a prong of rock sticking downward like a tusk from the overhang above him, and of course useless against a pull from any but the one, sideways, direction. Little J., who had by now begun his assorted collection of all our sacks and axes, followed up magnificently.

The next clear memory is of finding ourselves inside the second, smaller, chimney, a precipitous narrow cleft up the face, of worn, skull-smooth rock. It was all dirty white and bone-blue in the gloomy afternoon light, with blurred ice-nubbles bulking through the adhesive snow. But at least there was the singular rest for eye and nerves which the feeling of enclosing walls gives us after long hours on an exposed cliff. We even found a nominal stance or two, in ice-pockets on chockstones, where we could *almost* hold on without help from the hands. Franz, who was back again above me resting from the lead, could spare me a few partial hoists with the rope. I began to feel my muscles slackening with the relief, and I became conscious of the cold. I had time to notice that I was climbing less precisely, a symptom of relaxed tension: time, too, to admit ungrudgingly that nothing in the universe but Franz' rope could have got me up to and over some of the expulsive ice bulges in the chimney. Ignorant in my remote position of what the front men saw awaiting us above, I even thawed into a congratulatory remark or so: but I drew no response.

And then, it all ended! The chimney simply petered out: not under the south-east ridge, as we might have hoped, but in the very hard heart of the diamond precipice some six hundred feet [183 metres] below the final and still invisible summit. The vague exit from the chimney faded out against the base of a blank cliff. One of its side walls led on for a little, and up to the left. There it too vanished, under the lower rim of a big snowy slab, sloping up, and slightly conical, like a dish-cover. I have reason to remember that slab. It formed the repellent floor of a lofty, triangular recess. On its left side, and in front, there was space and ourselves. On its right, and at the back, a smooth leap of colossal cliff towered up for a hundred feet [30·5 metres] of crystallized shadow, and then arched out above our heads in a curve like the dark underside of a cathedral dome. A more appalling-looking finish to our grim battle of ascent could hardly have been dreamed in a 'falling' nightmare; and we had not even standing room to appreciate it worthily! As I looked up and down, I had an overpowering sense of the great grey wings behind us, shadowing suddenly close across the whole breadth of precipice, and folding us off finally from the world.

But our long apprenticeship to discouragement stood us in good stead. Muscles braced anew obstinately; determination quickened resentfully. The recess on whose lip we hung had been formed by the sliding of a great wedge of rock off the inclined, dish-cover slab, once its bed. But on our right the cliff continued the original line. My impression of this, therefore, was as of a high building viewed from under one corner. Its sheer front wall stretched away to the right, flush with the sill of our slab. The end wall of the building formed the right side of our recess, and overhung the slab. The rectangular house-corner, where the two walls joined, rose immediately above us, vertical and iced, but a little chipped by the rending out of the wedge. Again, the front wall of this projecting house did not rise to the same height as the cliff that backed our recess. Forty feet up [12 metres]—my measures are merely impressions—the wall slanted steeply back in a roof, receding out of sight. Presumably another huge wedge had here slid from its bed, on a higher plane. Above and beyond this roof the precipices rose again into sight, in the same line and of the same height as the cliffs which backed our recess. Only, the cliff vertically above us was crowned by the great dome or overhang. There must be, therefore, invisible above, some rough junction or flaw where the line of cliffs above the receding house-roof linked on to the forward jut of our dome. Four vital questions suggested themselves: Could the house-corner be climbed? Was the roof, if attainable, too steep to crawl up? Might there be a flawed connection where the precipice upon which the roof abutted joined on to the side of the dome? If there was such a flaw, would this yield us a passage out on to the face of the convex dome above its circle of largest dimension, on its retreating upper curve, or below it, under its hopeless arch? These details are tiresome, perhaps unintelligible. But they may help other climbers to a better understanding of Franz' remarkable feat.

Right up in the angle of the recess there was a rotund blister of rock modelled in low relief on the face of the slab; and round this a man, hunched on small nicks in the steep surface, could just belay the rope. Josef and Franz were crouching at this blister up in the recess. The rest of us were dispersed over freezing cling-holds along the lower rim of the slab. And the debate proceeded, broken by gusts of snow. The man to lead had clearly to run out a hundred to a hundred and fifty feet of rope [30·5 to 45·5 metres]. He could be given no protection. His most doubtful link would come some eighty feet up [24 metres] above the roof. If he found a flaw there, and it served him favourably, he would be out on the convex of the dome fully a hundred feet above us, and outside us in a direct line above our heads. If, at this point, he could not proceed—well, it was equally unlikely that he could return!

Franz showed no hesitation. The hampered preparations for the attempt went on hurriedly. We had all to unrope as best we could, so as to arrange for the two hundred feet [61 metres] of possible run-out, and we hooked on to our holds with difficulty, while the snow-frozen rope kinked and banged venomously about us. In the end little J. and I had to remain off the rope, to leave enough free.

Franz started up the corner, climbing with extraordinary nerve but advancing almost imperceptibly. It was much like swarming up the angle of a tower, rough-cast with ice. Ryan and little J. crept up near the blister; but as there was no more room I remained hanging on to the fractured sill of the slab. In this position I was farther out; and I could just see Franz' two feet scratting desperately for hold to propel him up the tilt of the roof above the corner. The rest of him was now out of sight. The minutes crawled like hours, and the rope hanging down to us over the gable-end hardly seemed to stir upwards. The snow gusts distracted us cruelly. A precipice in sunshine seems at least interested in our microscopic efforts. Its tranquillity even helps our movement by giving to it a conspicuous importance. But when the stable and unstable forces of nature join in one of their ferocious, inconclusive conflicts, the little human struggle is carelessly swallowed up in uproar, and tosses unregarded and morally deflated, like a wet straw on a volcanic wave.

Suddenly I heard that unmistakable scrape and grit of sliding boot-nails and clothes. Above my head, over the edge of the roof to the right, I saw Franz' legs shoot out into space. Time stopped. A shiver, like expectancy, trembled across the feeling of unseen grey wings behind me from end to end of the cliff. I realized impassively that the swirl of the rope must sweep me from my holds before it tightened on the doubtful belay of the blister. But fate was playing out the game in regions curiously remote. My mind watched the moves, itself absorbed into the same remote, dispassionate atmosphere. It seemed unwilling to disturb the issue by formulating a thought, or even a fear. The fact of the body seemed negligible; it had no part in the observant aloofness into which all consciousness had withdrawn. Something of the same feeling of separation between the body and the watching mind is the experience of men actually falling or drowning, when action is at an end and there is not even pain to reunite bodily and mental sensation. But during the crises of this day the condition lasted, with me certainly, for spaces that could only be measured by hours.

Franz' boots again disappeared above the edge. No one in the recess had known of the slip, out of their sight and lost in the gusts. He had stopped himself miraculously on the rim by crushing his hands on to ice-dimples in the slab. The hanging rope began again to travel up along the slanting gable-end of the roof. There was a long interval, and now and then the sound of a scratting boot or the scrabble of loose surface. Then the rope began, jerkily, to work out and across far above our heads. Franz had found a flaw in the join of the cliffs above the roof, and he was creeping out on to the projection of the dome. The lengthening rope now hung down well outside the men in the recess, and it might have hung outside me on the lower rim, had they not held in its end. Its weight upon Franz, as it swayed down through the snow, must have added to his immense difficulties. He was well out of sight, clinging somewhere above on the upper curve of the overhang.

An indistinct exchange of shouts began, half swallowed by echo, wind, and snow. Franz, it appeared, was still quite uncertain if he could get up any fuhrter. For the time he could hold on well enough to help one man with the rope; but he had not two hands free to pull. I could hear his little spurt of laughter at the question—'Could he return?' He suggested that Josef should join him, and the rest wait until they two might return with a rescue-party. Wait, there!—for at best fifteen hours, hanging on to the icy holds, in a snow wind!

At that hour of the day and upon those treacherous cliffs, now doubly dangerous under accumulating snow, all the odds were against any of us who turned back getting down alive. Franz in any case could not get back to us, and he might not be able to advance. We were committed, therefore, to the attempt to join him, however gloomy its outlook. As many as possible must be got up to him—and the rest must be left to chance.

Josef started his attempts on the corner. This left room for me to move up to Ryan on the slab. He asked me, I remember, what I thought were the chances of our escape. I remember, too, considering it seriously, and I can hear myself answering— 'About one in five.'

The end of the long rope hooted down past me. It hung outside the recess, dangling in air; and I could only recover it by climbing down again over the rim of the slab and reaching out for it one-handed with my axe. I passed it up; and then I stayed there, hanging on, because I could no longer trust my hands or feet to get me up the slope again. Ryan began the corner; but if I have described the position at all intelligibly, it will be seen that while the corner rose vertically on our right, the long rope hung down on a parallel line from the dome directly above our heads. So it came that the higher we climbed up the corner the more horizontal became the slanting pull of the rope, and the more it tended to drag us sideways off the corner and back under the overhang. Very coolly, Ryan shouted a warning before he started of the insufficient power left in frozen hands. Some twenty feet up [6 metres], the rope tore him from his inadequate, snowy holds. He swung across above our heads and hung suspended in mid-air. The rope was fixed round his chest. In a minute it began to suffocate him. He shouted once or twice to the men above to hurry. Then a fainter call, 'I'm done,' and he dangled to all appearance unconscious on the rope. Franz and Josef could only lift him half-inch by half-inch. For all this hour—probably it was longer—they were clamped one above the other on to the steep face of the dome, their feet on shallow but sound nicks, one hand clinging on, and only the other free to pull in. Any inch the one lifted, the other held. The rough curve of the rock, over which the higher portion of the rope descended, diminished by friction the effectiveness of each tug. The more one considers their situation, the more superhuman do the co-operation and power the two men displayed during this time, at the end of all those hours of effort, appear. Little J. and I had only the deadly anxiety of watching helplessly, staring upward into the dizzy snow and shadow: and that was enough. J. had followed silently and unselfishly the whole day; and even now he said nothing: crouching in unquestioning endurance beside the freezing blister on the slab.

Ryan was up at last, somehow, to the overhang; and being dragged up the rough curve above. A few small splinters were loosened, and fell, piping, past me and on to me. I remember calculating apathetically whether it was a greater risk to try and climb up again into the recess, unroped and without any feel in fingers and toes, or to stay where I was, hanging on to the sill, and chance being knocked off by a stone. It is significant of the condition of body and mind that I decided to stay where I was, where at least stiffened muscles and joints still availed to hold me mechanically fixed on to my group of rounded nicks.

Ryan was now out of sight and with the others. When the constriction of the rope was removed he must have recovered amazingly toughly, and at once; for down once more, after a short but anxious pause, whistled the snow-stiffened rope, so narrowly missing me that little J. cried out in alarm. I could not for a time hook it in with the axe; and while I stretched, frigidly and nervously, Josef hailed me from seemingly infinite height, his shouts travelling out on the snow eddies. They could not possibly pull up my greater weight. Unless I felt sure I could stick on to the corner and manage to climb round to them by Franz' route, it was useless my trying! At last I had fished in the rope, with a thrill of relief, and I set mental teeth. With those two tied on to the rope above, and myself tied on—in the way I meant to tie myself on—to the rope below, there were going to be no more single options. We were all in it together; and if I had still some faith in myself I had yet more in that margin of desperation strength which extends the possible indefinitely for such men as I knew to be linked on to me above. And if I were once up, well there would be no question after that about little J. coming up too!

I gave hands and feet a last blue-beating against the rock to restore some feeling to them. Then I knotted the rope round my chest, made the loose end into a triple-bowline 'chair' round my thighs, and began scratching rather futilely up the icy rectangular corner. For the first twenty-five feet [7·5 metres]— or was it much less?—I could just force upward. Then the rope began to drag me off inexorably. I clutched furiously up a few feet more; and then I felt I must let go, the drag was too strong for frozen fingers. As I had already resolved, at the last second I kicked off from the rock with all my strength. This sent me flying out on the rope, and across under the overhang, as if attached to a crazy pendulum. I could see J. crouching in the recess far below, instinctively protecting his head. The impetus jumped the upper part of the rope off its cling to the rock face of the dome above, and enabled the men to snatch in a foot or two. The return-swing brought me back, as I had half hoped, against the corner, a little higher up. I gripped it with fingers and teeth, and scrambled up another few feet. But the draw was now irresistible. I kicked off again; gained a foot or so, and spun back.

I was now up the corner proper, and I should have been by rights scrambling up the roof on the far side of my gable edge. But the rope, if nothing else, prevented any chance of my forcing myself over it and farther to the right. Another cling and scratch up the gable end, and I was not far below the level of the dome overhanging above and to my left. For the last time I fell off. This time the free length of the rope, below its hold upon the curve of the dome, was too short to allow of any return swing. So I shot out passively, to hang, revolving slowly, under the dome, with the feeling that my part was at an end. When I spun round inward, I looked up at the reddish, scarred wall freckled with snow, and at the tense rope, looking thin as a grey cobweb and disappearing fraily over the forespring of

rock that arched greedily over my head. When I spun outward,
I looked down—no matter how many thousand feet—to the
dim, shifting lines of the glacier at the foot of the peak, hazy
through the snowfall; and I could see, well inside my feet,
upon the dark face of the precipice the little blanched triangle
of the recess and the duller white dot of J.'s face as he crouched
by the blister. It flashed across me, absurdly, that he ought to
be more anxious about the effect of my gymnastics upon the
fragile thread of alpine rope, his one link with hope, than about
me!

I was quite comfortable in the chair; but the spinning had to
be stopped. I reached out the axe at full stretch, and succeeded
in touching the cliff, back under the overhang. This stopped me,
face inward. I heard inarticulate shouting above, and guessed
its meaning, although I was now too close under the dome to
catch the words:—'They could not lift my dead weight!' I
bethought me, and stretched out the axe again; got its point
against a wrinkle of the wall, and pushed out. This started me
swinging straight out and in below the dome. After two pokes I
swung in near enough to be able to give a violent, short-armed
thrust against the cliff. It carried me out far enough to jump quite
a number of feet of rope clear of its cling down the rock above.
The guides took advantage of the easing to haul in, and I
pendulum'd back a good foot higher. The cliff facing me was
now beginning to spring out in the Gothic arch of the overhang; so it could be reached more easily. I repeated the shove-out
more desperately. Again they hauled in on the released rope.
This time I came back close under the arch; and choosing a spot
as I swung in, I lifted both feet, struck them at the wall, and gave
a convulsive upward and outward spring. The rope shortened
up; and as I banged back the cornice of the arch loomed very
near above my head. But the free length of rope below it was
now too short to let me again reach to the back of the arch
with leg or axe. I hung, trying in vain to touch the lowest
moulding of the cornice above with my hands. I heard gasps
and grunts above quite distinctly now. The rope strained and
creaked, gritting over the edge of the rock above me. I felt the
tremor of the sinews heaving on it. But for all that, I did not
move up. I reached up with the axe in both hands, just hooked
the pick into a lucky chink of the under-moulding, and pulled,
with a frantic wriggle of the whole body. It was a feeble lift,

but enough for the sons of Anak above to convert into a valuable gain. The axe slipped down on to my shoulder, held there by its sling. I reached up and back with both arms, got hold of a finger-grip and gained another inch. Infinitesimal inches they seemed, each a supreme effort, until my nose and chin scratched up against a fillet of the cornice. Then the arms gave out completely, so much at the end of their strength that they dropped lifeless. But the teeth of the upper jaw held on a broken spillikin and, with the stronger succour of the rope, supported me for the seconds while the blood was running back into my arms.

Wrestle by wrestle it went on. Every reserve of force seemed exhausted, but the impulse was now supplied by a flicker of hope. Until, at last, I felt my knee catch over a moulding on the edge, and I could sink for an instant's rest, with rucked clothes clinging over the rough, steep, upward but *backward* curving of the dome. It is impossible to suggest the relief of that feeling, the proof that the only solid surface which still kept me in touch with existence had ceased to thrust itself out for ever as a barrier overhead, and was actually giving back below me in semi-support.

But there was no time, or inclination, to indulge panting humanity with a rest or a realization. I crept up a few feet, on to small, brittle, but sufficient crinkles. The dark figures of the three men above were visible now, clinging crab-like and exhausted on to similar nicks, indistinct in the snow dusk, but still human company. I had to stay where I was, and untie my rope, knotting up a coil at the end of the heavy length so that I could swing it inward to little J. back and out of sight beneath me in the recess. The second cast was true: I felt him handle it, and then I let it go for those in the more direct line above to hold. Presently I saw it writhing away from me across the few visible feet of stooping crag, as J. below moved away to start the icy corner. He had, I think, two sacks beside his own and at least three extra axes slung on to him; but he grappled up the corner masterfully and forced his way out on to the roof. Hopeless of lifting him as they had lifted us, the men above had learned, from pure fatigue, to leave him more free upon the rope. But he was naturally a very long time; and there was all too much leisure in which to realize how irrevocably our descent was now cut off, and how improbably our ascent could be continued.

The first flare of blinding relief died down. The obscure future settled round again like a fog. The precipice receding into murky uncertainty above looked more than ever dark with discouragement for a vitality ebbing on the tide of reaction. The shadowy, humping figures above were silent; there was none of that heartening talk which greets us over a difficult edge, giving us assurance that the worst is past. With no longer even the rope about me as a reminder of companionship, the sense that others were near me and in like case passed out of mind. My thoughts wandered drowsily, and all life in the limbs seemed suspended, as we feel it to be sometimes in the moments just preceding sleep.

The snow began to fall in large, soft flakes; not the tingling darts that assail us with the crisp hostility of intruders upon our alien earth, but flakes like wings, instinct with life, surrounding and welcoming a visitor to their own region of air with vague but insistent friendliness. A few of them settled inquisitively, to gleam and fade for a second like fallen star-light, on the short arc of brown crag racing into shadow between my feet. The rest drifted lightly and recklessly down past my heels, to disappear over the rim of void: suggesting how easy and restful might be my own descent could tired muscles but be persuaded to relax their tenacious hold upon the few remaining feet of inhospitable rock. Far below and to the right, a brow of bending and frosted precipice frowned into sight; and against and round its more familiar obstruction, lit by a pale glare diffused through the low clouds, the white flakes twirled and circled intimately, already forgetful of their more timid flight past the stranger above. When they sank from it, it was into an immensity of grey haze, featureless but for the black ribbons of moraine which floated high and distinct above their unseen glaciers, as reeds seem to sway and float high over the reflecting depths of a transparent stream. Into these immeasurably grey depths everything seemed to be descending, unresistingly and as of choice—the long lines of ice-fast crag, the shifting eddies of snow, the rays of darkness under the storm-clouds, even the eye and the tired mind. Some rebellious instinct of hand and foot alone appeared to defy a universal law.

The appearance of little J. as he clambered, a clattering brown goblin of sack-humps and axe-points, over a boss on the shadowy dome beside me brought me back to the world of human company, and struggle. The day was darkening steadily—or is my memory of darkness only the shadow of our circumstance? for it was not yet four o'clock: but the snow stopped, having done its worst where it could most impede us. We roped up patiently, and began again our age-long crawl and halt up icy slabs as little kindly as before; and every fifty feet [15 metres] above us loomed still the threat of a total interruption. If it came now—it must just come! We had none of us, I think, any apprehension left: or for that matter, any comprehension of much more than hanging on and forcing up. In my own case— and a truthful record of sensation limits me to thinking only of myself—the capacity to feel or to remark was exhausted. Franz must have been more nervously alert, for he ground out a devious upward line through the upheaving of giant slabs without a halt or a false attempt. I can recall nothing but obscurity, steepness, and an endless driving of the muscles to their task. Still no message of hope reached us from above; and yet we must have left another four hundred feet [122 metres] of rib and crack, snow-ice and equivocal holds below us. Even fancy dared not whisper to itself of the summit: the next five feet, and still the next five feet were the end of all effort and expectation.

And then, something was happening! There came a mutter of talk from the dusk above. Surely two shadows were actually moving at one time? I was at the foot of a long icy shelf, slanting up to the right. It was overhung by cliff on the left, as usual; and it had the usual absence of any holds to keep me on it. I began the eternal knee-friction crawl. The rope tightened on my waist. 'Shall I pull?'—called Josef's voice, sounding strange after the hours of silence, and subdued to an undertone as if he feared that the peak might still hear and wake up to contrive some new devilment. 'Why not?—if you really can!'—I echoed, full of surprise and hope; and I skimmered up the trough, to find Josef yoked to a royal rock hitch, the third and the best of the day! And, surely, we were standing on the crest of a great ridge, materialized as if by magic out of the continuous darkness of cliff and sky? And the big, sullen shadow just above must be the summit! It was indeed the mounting edge of the south-east ridge upon which we had arrived; and sixty feet [18 metres] above us it curled over against the top of the final pyramid. Josef unroped from me, while I brought up little J.; and as we started to finish the ascent together in our old-time partnership,

I saw the silhouettes of the other three pass in succession over the pointed skyline of the peak.

We found them, relaxed in spent attitudes on the summit-slabs, swallowing sardines and snow, our first food since half-past seven in the morning. It was now close upon six o'clock. Franz came across to meet me, and we shook hands. 'You will never do anything harder than that, Franz!' 'No,' he said reflectively, 'man could not do much more.'

4
Nanda Devi

ERIC SHIPTON

Eric Shipton, who played a leading part in paving the way which led to the eventual climbing of Everest, was not only a fine mountaineer but also an explorer par excellence. His urge was to search in the unmapped corners of the globe; his happiness resided in the remote security which mountains can give to human beings. Like many of us, he most enjoyed travelling simply and with few companions; he demonstrated the merits of lightly equipped expeditions in East Africa, the Himalayas, the Karakoram and Patagonia. Like Geoffrey Young's, his record of those experiences will continue to be a source of inspiration to many future climbers and explorers.

The author is describing how he and H. W. Tilman, with their Sherpa companions Pasang, Angtarkay and Kusang, set out with Dhotial porters to force their way through a narrow and precipitous gorge, the Rishi Ganga, to reach the 'sanctuary' at the foot of a high Himalayan peak, Nanda Devi, which at that time had not been climbed.

For the best part of two days we fought our way through soft snow up to our knees, our waists and occasionally up to our armpits. Tilman and I, lightly laden, went ahead to flog the trail, while the others struggled along behind with their enormous loads. Twice, after exhausting effort, we reached a saddle which we hoped was the pass, only to find a sheer drop of several thousand feet on the other side. The third time we were lucky.

Once in the valley beyond the pass, we descended below the spring snow-line, and life was more comfortable. But the huge scale of the country made route-finding very difficult, and over and over again we reached an impasse and were forced to retreat to try another line. This was terribly disheartening for the Dhotials, but they stuck to it splendidly. As we went, their loads became lighter by the amount of food that was eaten and by the dumps of tsampa which we left each day for their return journey.

It was a most magnificent place. The southern side of the valley was built up of tier upon tier of gigantic, steeply inclined slabs, which culminated 10,000 feet [3,050 metres] above the river in a multitude of sharp rock spires set at a rakish angle, while beyond them stood great ice peaks. The northern side, along which we were travelling, was broken up into a series of glens. Some of these contained little alps, each a fairy garden of birch and pine trees, deep grass and drifts of flowers aflame with colour, each secluded from the savage world outside by precipice and crag.

Unfortunately, we had little 'time to stand and stare', for now we had a fresh reason for haste. The Dhotials had to be fed, and each day we spent in getting to the Rhamani junction meant that we would have three days' less food for the work beyond. We were by no means certain of inducing them to go as far. As we advanced, 'the valley grew narrow and narrower still', and its sides became steeper and steeper. The Dhotials liked the look of it not at all. Their protests became stronger and more difficult to overcome. Mercifully the weather held; a single day of mist, rain or snow would have stopped us, and we would have been faced with the laborious task of relaying the loads the rest of the way to our base by ourselves. Actually, in spite of our many mistakes and setbacks, and by driving the unfortunate Dhotials through all the daylight hours, we covered the distance in the time allotted—six days from the Dhauli river—and arrived at the Rhamani junction by nightfall on May 28th. To emphasise our good fortune, a storm which had been brewing for some time past broke five minutes before we had found a suitable site for our base camp, and heavy snow fell throughout the night.

The next morning we paid the Dhotials the reward they had so richly deserved, and parted with them on the best of terms.

They expressed reluctance at leaving us alone in such a fearsome spot, and we for our part were very sorry to see them go, for they had served us well, and we had become very fond of them.

I have never been able to decide whether, in mountain exploration, it is the prospect of tackling an unsolved problem, or the performance of the task itself, or the retrospective enjoyment of successful effort, which affords the greatest amount of pleasure. Each provides emotions so widely different, each has its particular limiting factor—restless uncertainty, fear or fatigue, or regret for an enchanting problem that is no more. Certainly no situation has provided me with greater happiness than that in which we found ourselves at the mouth of the upper gorge of the Rishi Ganga. Four miles of canyon, one of the mightiest in

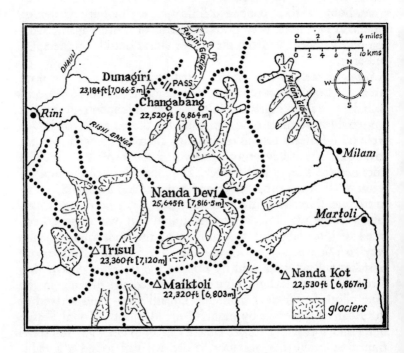

Map of the area around Nanda Devi

the world, separated us from the untrodden country beyond. We had sufficient food to last us for five weeks. Whether we succeeded or failed, nothing but a bad accident could deprive us of some of the best weeks of our lives.

Our base camp was on a narrow strip of shore, covered with birch jungle, on the southern side of the river. The cliffs, undercut by the action of water, provided us with a snug cave. It was a very pleasant spot for temporary residence; though the lack of sunlight, the sense of confinement and the thunder of the river, amplified by echo, might have become irksome had we been forced to stay there long. The immediate prospect was far from encouraging. A few yards beyond the strip of shore the river issued from a perfect box-canyon, whose vertical sides were smooth and almost unbroken. However, a little gully above the camp enabled us to climb beyond the overhanging cliffs to easier ground. Two thousand feet [610 metres] above the river we reached the first of a series of broken terraces which ran along the side of the gorge.

It took us nine days to find a way and to relay our food and equipment through the remaining four miles of the gorge. It was exhilarating work, for until the last moment the issue was in doubt, and each section of our route appeared to rely for its practicability upon the slender chance of a rock fault. Apart from the immense scale of the precipices, the weight of our loads precluded any really difficult climbing, except in short vertical sections where the baggage could be hauled up on the rope. The last mile of the gorge looked so unpromising that we tried to force our way up the river bed itself by zig-zagging from side to side. This attempt provided our most exciting adventure as the force of the current was terrific. It was perhaps fortunate that it did not succeed, for later, as the ice of the glaciers started to melt more rapidly, the river became very swollen, and we would certainly not have succeeded in getting back that way. Defeated there, Pasang and I then tried to find a way along the northern side of the gorge, while Tilman and Angtarkay explored the remainder of the southern side. We failed to make any headway, but the other two discovered the last frail link of the chain, and we entered the Nanda Devi basin with enough food for three weeks.

We set about our task of exploring the basin with a feeling of great exultation. After the confinement of the gorge, the freedom of movement about wide open country was a delicious contrast. The exquisite joy that any mountaineer must experience in treading new ground lent a special charm to everything we did and saw; even our clumsy toil with the plane-table yielded deep satisfaction as a form of self-expression. It was glorious country; gentle moorland grazed by herds of bharal (wild sheep), and in places gay with Alpine flowers; small lakes that reflected the surrounding mountains; deep lateral valleys holding glaciers, enclosed by a hundred magnificent peaks of clean, strong granite or glistening ice and snow. Out of the centre of the basin rose the wonderful spire of Nanda Devi 13,000 feet [3,965 metres] above its base, peerless among mountains, always changing and ever more lovely with each new aspect, each fresh effect of colour and cloud.

Three weeks was not long enough to explore the whole of the basin, so we decided to concentrate upon the northern half, and to return to survey the southern half in September, when the monsoon should be over. This plan had an additional advantage, as we wished to find another way out, over one of the ranges that formed the 'rim' of the basin; to have done so now would have interfered with our programme for the monsoon season in the Badrinath range to the north. We had many more fine days than bad, and the weather seldom hindered us. We rarely bothered to pitch a tent, as we found it so much pleasanter to sleep in the open, even at our higher camps. It seemed somehow to provide a continuity between rest and action, to deepen the sense of harmony between ourselves and our surroundings, which even the thin canvas walls of a tent can destroy. In the lower parts of the basin there was a plentiful supply of juniper wood, and there we had the luxury of huge camp fires. Higher up we had to be more economical, though we generally managed to carry some wood up with us so as to avoid using a stove. Though we were concerned mainly with exploring and mapping the country, we were able to combine this with some mountaineering on the higher peaks. We reached three saddles on the western and northern 'rim' of the basin, each more than 20,000 feet high [6,096 metres]. We climbed a peak of 21,000 feet [6,400 metres], and made an unsuccessful attempt to climb another of about 23,000 feet [7,010 metres]. On each occasion we had wonderful views of the basin itself and over the ranges outside it.

The monsoon came gradually towards the end of June, and its arrival coincided with the exhaustion of our food supplies. Meagre dumps had been left at various places in the Rishi Ganga. We returned down the gorge in torrential rain; tussles with the swollen waters of the river and of side streams provided the main excitement. The gorge was even more impressive in foul weather than in fair. Particularly I remember one night of heavy storm. I was snugly wedged in a little recess between two boulders listening comfortably to the hiss of the rain outside, and to the thunder which, echoing along miles of crag, maintained an almost unbroken roll. Lightning flickered continuously upon the grim precipices and upon cloud banners entwined about buttress and corrie. The sense of fantasy was heightened by the semi-consciousness of a fitful sleep. At one moment it seemed that I was perched on an eagle's nest above an infernal cauldron of infinite depth, at another that I was floating with the mist, myself a part of an unearthly tempest.

July and August were spent in exploring the range of mountains which forms the watershed between the three main sources of the Ganges. It is a country full of romantic legend. Most of this is rather difficult to follow without a deep study of Hindu mythology, but mountain legend is always fascinating. Our chief object was to link up the three main affluents of the Ganges, the rivers Alaknanda, Bhagirathi and Mandakini, by passes leading across the range direct from one to another.

The determination of the actual source of a great river is often a matter for conjecture, since the choice may lie between streams with various claims to the title. First there is the traditional source, ascribed by ancient history or local legend. An example of this kind is to be found in Ptolemy's remarkable statement that the Nile was born of two small, bottomless wells situated in the 'Mountains of the Moon'—a statement made nearly two thousand years before any recorded visit to the upper reaches of the Nile. Dr Humphreys discovered in Ruwenzori two tiny lakes of immense depth which gave rise to a stream which formed part of the head-waters of the great river. Some Hindu mythology ascribes the source of the Ganges to a beautiful waterfall which forms a tiny tributary of the Alaknanda river. Modern geography demands a more concrete claim: the stream which rises the farthest in a direct line from the river's mouth;

the stream whose waters travel the greatest distance; the source that supplies the greatest volume of water.

There is nothing in my experience more fascinating than finding and crossing an unknown pass across a mountain range. The more important the watershed, geographically speaking, the more satisfying is the achievement, but even the crossing of a minor pass can be an exciting experience. To my mind it is mountaineering at its best, for it combines in even measure so many branches of the craft: accurate appreciation of the country as a whole, judgment of difficulty, anticipation of unknown factors, technical skill and disposal of resources. Then there is the eager speculation upon the difficulties of the other side, the thrilling moment when these are revealed and the enchanting descent into the new world beyond. The view, too, from a pass is often much more satisfying than that from a high peak, for, though less comprehensive, it reveals the surroundings more in their true perspective: the mountains are not dwarfed, and there is not the same mass of jumbled detail.

Our first plan was to cross the range from Badrinath to the Gangotri glacier, the largest in the Central Himalayas, to explore its unknown upper reaches and to work our way down to the source of the Bhagirathi at its foot. In 1912, C. F. Meade and his two Alpine guides had reached the watershed from the Bhagat Kharak glacier, but they had not descended to the other side of the range. This was therefore the obvious way of approach. But when we reached its foot we judged that the route to Meade's saddle was in danger of being swept by ice avalanches from the peaks above. In this I think we were mistaken. However, as there seemed to be no alternative route across the main watershed from the upper basin of the Bhagat Kharak, we crossed a series of passes to the north. This led us eventually into the glacier system above the Arwa valley, where we had spent a fortnight after climbing Kamet, three years before. From there we crossed the main watershed and descended a long tributary which joined the Gangotri glacier only two or three miles above its snout. We went on down to the source of the river, and then returned over the range to Badrinath.

These activities occupied us during most of July, and at the beginning of August we started on the second half of our monsoon programme. This proved to be considerably more exacting than the other. Our plan was to cross the range, this time from

Badrinath to Kedarnath, another famous Hindu shrine. No route was known to exist across the range between these two places, but among the many legends of the country was a story that many hundred years ago there was no high priest of Kedarnath Temple, and that the high priest of Badrinath used to hold services in the temples of both places on the same day. The tradition of the lost pass is a common one in mountains of Central Asia.

From the head of the Satopanth glacier we reached a saddle, 18,400 feet high [5,610 metres], on the crest of the main watershed. We arrived there in thick mist and falling snow, but on the following morning there was a brief clearing which revealed a discouraging view of the other side. The glacier forming our saddle descended in a steep ice-fall for about a thousand feet [305 metres], then it flattened out into a fairly level stretch of ice before heeling over for a final tremendous plunge into the blue depths of a gorge 6,000 feet [1,830 metres] beneath us. We began to have a healthy respect for our reverend predecessor.

After some search we managed to find a way down through the first ice-fall on to the terrace. But the next part of the problem was much more formidable. The angle of the ice below increased steadily, and it soon appeared that we were on the upper part of a hanging glacier. We worked over to the right and descended for a few hundred feet before we were brought up by an impassable crevasse. Then we tried on the left, and on the following morning succeeded in roping down into a narrow gully between the ice and the containing rock wall of the glacier.

The forest-filled valley below appeared very enticing from the icy steep above, but when eventually we reached it we soon changed our opinion. The undergrowth in the forest was so dense and the sides of the valley so steep that we could rarely cover more than a mile a day. Side streams, too, caused us a lot of trouble, for they were generally at the bottom of deep ravines and always in spate. One of these held us up for two days before we found a place at which we could bridge it. It rained incessantly and with considerable vigour, so that our loads soon became waterlogged. This precipitated a crisis in the food situation. We had already spent longer over the job than we had anticipated, and now our small supply of tsampa had become as sodden as everything else, despite the fact that it was packed in canvas bags. It went bad, and we suffered such acute stomach-ache when we ate it in this condition that we jettisoned the remainder. To add to our troubles, a falling rock hit Pasang on the foot and, I think, broke a small bone, so that he could only just get along without a load, and from then on was no more than a passenger.

The main concern of the Sherpas was their fear of bears. Having no experience of Himalayan bears, Tilman and I were able to take the menace more calmly. Actually we only encountered one of the creatures at close quarters, and he ambled off as soon as we came upon him round a corner. That we did not meet more was probably due to the din the Sherpas made as we went along, designed to scare them away, for their spoor was everywhere. But the bears were a nuisance in that they were our rivals in the difficult matter of feeding.

We owed our salvation, or at least the fact that we did not land ourselves in a considerably worse mess, largely to the woodcraft of the Sherpas. First and foremost they provided us with food by their knowledge of edible plants. Our staple diet was bamboo shoots. This delicacy only occurs in its edible form for a short season of the year, and it was fortunate for us that it was then in season. The shoots were anything up to eight feet long [2·5 metres], but only an inch or so below each notch was edible. However, except where a hungry bear had forestalled us, it was fairly easy to collect a potful of the little green cylinders, which, boiled, constituted our evening meal. It was quite a good dish; with a little imagination, not unlike asparagus. But, though the shoots could also be eaten raw as we went along, they were insubstantial food to sustain the long hours of heavy physical labour that our progress demanded. Once we found a fairly large quantity of an edible forest fungus. Boiled, it had the negative taste of overstewed meat, but it was pleasantly satisfying.

Each night Angtarkay and Kusang displayed considerable skill in constructing a bamboo shelter under which we could light a fire. On the first night this appeared to me an impossible undertaking, but it was not beyond the ingenuity of the Sherpas. By pounding some sodden sticks of dead bamboo with a stone, and holding the pulp over a series of lighted matches, it eventually took the flame. This was fed by more dead bamboo until there was a sufficient blaze to dry and ignite logs of wood, and in a

couple of hours we would have a good fire. Fortunately we had
a large supply of matches that had been safely stowed in a pair
of sheepskin gauntlets. We halted at about five o'clock each
evening so as to give ourselves time to construct a platform if
necessary, to build the shelter and light a fire under it and to
collect bamboo shoots and fuel. After that we would strip off
our sodden garments and roast our naked bodies by the fire
until we went to sleep.

The work during the day was rather exasperating. An endless
succession of rocky, bramble-filled gullies made the going
exceedingly slow and laborious, so that frequently it took us an
hour to cover twenty-five yards [23 metres]. In some places a
cliff or ravine would force us to climb many hundreds of feet.
We had to maintain our altitude so as to avoid getting out of
the bamboo zone. But in other places the going was good, and
the day's toil generally yielded about a mile of progress.

Apart from the problem of food, which was worrying, it
was not on the whole an unpleasant experience; the days were
full of vital interest, the nights warm and comfortable, and the
forest was wild and beautiful. Anyway, whatever discomforts
and anxieties were our portion, these were amply repaid when
at length we reached a tiny hamlet consisting of three houses
and some fields. The hamlet provided us with a dry billet in a
barn, four pounds of flour, a cucumber, some dry apricots and
the happy knowledge that our struggle with the forest was at
an end and that a well-worn path would lead on down the
valley to the Kedarnath pilgrim route.

In September we went up the Rishi Ganga again. The difference
between this and our previous journey was even more striking
than the difference between the first and second ascents of a
peak, for the size of the valley had laid more emphasis upon the
problem of finding a route than upon actual difficulties. We had
covered the ground so often in the process of relaying loads and
knew so exactly what lay round each corner and how long each
section would take, that now it was hard to believe that we
had experienced any difficulty on the first occasion. For once I
was keeping a day-to-day diary, and it was interesting to read
over the entries made on the first occasion. This time we were
only two days getting through the upper part of the gorge
from the Rhamani junction, and we took local men with us
right through into the Nanda Devi basin before we discharged

them and sent them back. By then the monsoon was spent and we had a long spell of fine weather.

The geography of the southern section of the basin was simple and our rough plane-table survey of it did not take long. First we set out to climb a peak (since named Maiktoli), 22,320 feet high [6,805 metres], and situated on the southern 'rim' of the basin. We pitched a camp at 20,000 feet [6,100 metres], but just before we reached this point Tilman became ill with 'mountain sickness' and had to return with Pasang. The following day, Kusang, Angtarkay and I climbed the peak, from which we had a most magnificent view. Even the gigantic southern face of Nanda Devi was dwarfed by the very extent of the panorama. The Badrinath peaks, Kamet, the Kosa group, Dunagiri and the great peaks of the northern part of the Nanda Devi basin, all mountains amongst which we had been travelling for the past four months, served merely as a foil to set off the stupendous ranges lying beyond Milam and across the borders of Western Nepal. What a wonderful field of exploration lay there—the heritage of some future generation.

Tilman, for all his strength and mountaineering competence, appeared to be quite unable to acclimatize to high altitudes. It seemed that his ceiling was about 20,000 or 21,000 feet [6,100 or 6,400 metres], and on the several occasions when we went above that altitude he became ill. Though he was supremely fit, he was no better in this respect at the end of the season than he was at the beginning.

One of our chief interests on our second visit to the basin was to find a route by which Nanda Devi could be climbed. The northern side, which we had seen on our first visit, was utterly impregnable and the great western ridge scarcely less so. This left two alternatives: firstly, an ascent of the east peak of the mountain from the south, and thence along the crest of a tremendous curtain of rock, two miles long, to the main peak: secondly, a route up the great south ridge of the main peak. The former we ruled out owing to its immense length and to the appearance of the connecting ridge, which was serrated and probably knife-sharp, and which maintained an altitude of some 24,000 feet [7,315 metres] throughout. But the south ridge, though formidable, was by no means hopeless. It swept up in a great curve from the floor of the basin at about 17,000 feet [5,180 metres] to the summit, 25,660 feet [7,820 metres]. Though steep it maintained a fairly uniform angle and was broad enough to allow the choice of alternative routes up its difficult sections. Its great advantage was that there was no long and complicated approach, and that its base was within easy reach of juniper fuel, so that it could be reached by porters without special high-altitude equipment.

With only two tents, one Primus stove and very little kerosene, our boots full of holes and now almost devoid of nails, we were obviously in no position to make a serious attempt to climb Nanda Devi. But we could at least climb some way up the ridge and get a pretty good idea of the nature of the difficulties. We camped near its foot on a little alp covered with grass and snowy edelweiss, and on the following day climbed some 3,000 feet [915 metres] up the ridge. We would have had time to go farther but Tilman again felt the effects of the altitude and began to vomit. But we had gone far enough to see that the ridge was practicable. We had encountered no serious difficulties, and though there might be plenty ahead, the uniform angle of the ridge and its width made it unlikely that any of these would prove to be insurmountable by a thoroughly competent party. It would be no easy task, and, in my judgment, not one for a large, heavily organized expedition. But what a prize! There is no finer mountain in the world. Its graceful beauty from every aspect was a source of inspiration and wonder as the Matterhorn had been to Alpine mountaineers in the middle of the nineteenth century. And what finer setting than a hitherto inviolate sanctuary?

Finally we set about the achievement of our long-cherished ambition, to find an exit from the basin over some portion of its 'rim'. The southern segment offered us two alternatives. One was a saddle reached by Longstaff and his guides in 1905 in their attempt to reach the basin from the east, the other was a depression on the southern 'rim', which Ruttledge and his guide, Emile Rey, had attempted in 1932. Both these ways were likely to prove extremely difficult. At first we were inclined to favour 'Longstaff's Col', for he had proved the practicability of its farther side by climbing it from that direction; also it was the lower of the two. But its western aspect looked so formidable that we decided to attempt the Sunderdhunga Col, as the southern saddle was called. We had seen that we could reach it easily from the north, but Ruttledge's description of its southern aspect was far from encouraging: 'Six thousand feet [1,830 metres] of the steepest rock and ice. . . . Near the top of the wall, for about a mile and a half, runs a terrace of ice some two hundred feet thick [60 metres]; in fact the lower edge of a hanging glacier. Under the pull of gravity large masses constantly break off from this terrace and thunder down into the valley below, polishing in their fall the successive bands of limestone precipice of which the face is composed. Even supposing the precipice to be climbable, an intelligent mountaineer may be acquitted on a charge of lack of enterprise if he declines to spend at least three days and two nights under fire from this artillery. An alternative is the choice of three knife-edge arêtes, excessively steep in their middle and lower sections, on which even the eye of faith, assisted by binoculars, fails to see a single platform large enough to accommodate the most modest of climbing tents.'

I had seen something of this precipice from the summit of Maiktoli which stood immediately above the saddle, and the view confirmed Ruttledge's description. But it is a very different matter to get down such a place carrying a small quantity of food, and to force a way up it with the prospect of being cut off for weeks from further supplies. We should be able to move much more rapidly over the danger areas, and to rope down ice-cliffs and other obstacles that might otherwise have been impossible or very difficult to climb; though of course we should be handicapped in the choice of a route. Anyway, we decided to give it a trial, and leaving a dump of food in the basin against our probable failure, made our way to the saddle.

We reached it one morning and spent the rest of the day trying, in bad visibility, to find a point from which to start the descent. First we tried to reach the rock arêtes or ridges that Ruttledge had referred to as being out of range of the ice avalanches from the hanging-glacier terrace. We could see the top of the first one through the mist on our left, but we could not reach it. Then we tried to the right, but were brought up short on the brink of the ice terrace overhanging the ice-polished limestone cliffs that plunged out of sight. It was a fine spectacle. Every now and then enormous masses of ice would break away from the cliffs on which we were standing and crash with a thunderous roar into the cloudy depths below. It is not often that one has the opportunity of watching a display of ice avalanches from so close, and rarer still to see them breaking away from the very cliffs on which one is standing.

Our only alternative now was a narrow ice-fall lying between the terrace and the three arêtes, and of which we could see no more than a few feet of twisted and riven ice. There was nothing to do but to go straight for it and worry our way down by a tedious process of trial and error. However, we had plenty of food with us, and so long as we could keep out of the line of bombardment from the terrace we could afford to take several days over the job if necessary. It was strenuous work trying line after line without success, but as the evening wore on our energy seemed to increase—a phenomenon I have often noticed in mountaineering. A series of slender ice bridges suspended over space by some conjuring trick of nature would lead us downwards to the brink of an impassable chasm. Then a wearisome retreat by the way we had come, to try a new and perhaps equally futile chance. The farther we went the more complex became the precipitous maze we were in.

The next morning we waited until the sun was up before starting again, as our clothes had become sodden in the soft snow of the previous day and an early start would probably have resulted in frostbite. It was a most lovely dawn. In the right and left foreground were the icy walls, steep-sided and grim, enclosing the head of the Maiktoli valley; in front, beyond the brink of the ice ledge on which we were camped, and immensely far below, was a lake of vivid colour, at the bottom of which we could see the Sunderdhunga, coiling like a silver water-snake, away into a placid cloud-sea which stretched without a break over the foothills and the plains of India.

The day was one of vivid life and heavy toil. Hour after hour we puzzled and hacked our way down, lowering our loads and ourselves on the rope down an ice cliff, chipping laboriously across the steep face of a tower or along a knife-edged crest, sometimes hopeful and sometimes despairing. The ice-fall stood out in high relief from the mountainside, so that we were fairly well protected from the ice avalanches, which started falling again in the heat of the afternoon. Evening found us working on dry ice 3,000 feet down [915 metres], and it was becoming increasingly clear that we must soon find a way off the glacier, which evidently overhung at its base. Beside us to our right was a prominent rock ridge, which, though lying immediately below the higher line of hanging glaciers, offered us a heaven-sent alternative if only we could reach it. We cut steps to the edge of the glacier and from there we looked down a 60-foot ice-cliff [18-metre] into a steep gully of polished slabs. It was obviously a path for ice avalanches, but it was narrow and once in it we could cross to the farther side in a couple of minutes. By chipping away the ice in a circle we fashioned a bollard, from which we roped down the wall into the gully. A short race across it took us to a little ledge under an overhang on the ridge, which offered a convenient and well-protected site for a camp. No sooner had we pitched the tents than there came a mighty roar from above and for fully a minute a cascade of huge ice-blocks crashed down the gully sending up a spray of ice dust, while a number of ice splinters landed harmlessly on the tents.

The day, begun with the sight of a dawn beautiful beyond description and crowded with lively experience, closed with us stretched luxuriously on our ledge, perched high up amongst the precipitous glaciers of one of the grandest of mountain cirques. Lightning flickered somewhere in the east; the distant thunder was almost indistinguishable from the growl of avalanches. Mists floated stealthily in and out of corries above us, forming and dissolving in an ever-changing pattern. Far to the south a placid sea of cloud still stretched over the foot-hills, and the silvery light of a full moon lent to the scene an appearance of infinite depth. It was our last high camp that year, for by the evening of the following day we had reached the foot of the precipice and we slept that night on grassy meadowland.

Our exit from the sanctuary by way of the Sunderdhunga Col provided a fitting climax to our season of joyous freedom and high mountain adventure—the best five months that either of us had known. We considered the idea of setting out on some new project, but autumn was already well advanced, boots were ragged and funds running low; the break had to be faced sometime, and the perfection of the whole might be spoilt by some minor or uncompleted venture. So we set our course for home.

The march back added a rich store of memories: a struggle to find an exit from the grim gorge in the Upper Sunderdhunga valley, into which we had blundered in a heavy mist; our last encounter with a swollen mountain torrent; an enormous feast of wild raspberries and Himalayan blackberries lower down the valley; the generous hospitality of the first villagers we met, and the sweetness of their honey; the sparkling sunlit mornings as we lay sleepily watching the smoke of some distant wood fire mounting straight up into the clear air above the pine forest; a dawn on the distant ice-clad giants whose presence we had just left.

5

Via Della Pera

GRAHAM BROWN

Like Geoffrey Young before the First World War, Graham Brown in the 1920s was a climber who nearly always climbed with guides in the Western Alps. It was his daring eye for a route, which some outstanding professionals of that period were bold and skilful enough to lead, which produced another marvellous combination on the mountains. No one who has viewed the southern ramparts of Mont Blanc, towering above the valleys which lead down into Italy, can fail to be impressed by the fact that several of the most difficult and direct ways to the top of Europe's highest mountain were forced more than forty years ago. Having sampled two of them myself, and having known the man, I can bear testimony to the dogged tenacity of Graham Brown. He is here describing the most difficult of the three routes up the Brenva Face in whose first ascents he took a leading part. All these climbs start from a depression in a snow arête which ends at the foot of the Face—the Col Moore.

It was well behind our projected time when we reached the crest of Col Moore at 3.10 a.m., in just less than two and a half hours of movement from the Torino hut.

We did not pause, but at once went forward to repeat the horizontal traverse made on 26th July. The first steep couloir, which is really an extension of the South-West flank of Col Moore under the terminal cliff of the buttress on the old Brenva route, was a little awkward in the dim light, and it was now iced, so that this passage occupied twenty-five minutes. An ascent at the far side brought us to the near edge of the second couloir or snow-slope on the way to the Sentinelle—that with the ice run in the middle. This slope, set at an angle of 30° or so, terminates above a precipice which plunges steeply to the West bay of the Brenva Glacier. Down the near edge we went, but diverging from it, until we came a little short of the foot of the slope. Then we went forward horizontally and crossed the ice run where it had splayed out and was almost indistinguishable. Here we began to enter upon the Brenva face, and as our way took us along snow and then in rocks, the silence of the night gripped me. Far below on our left was the surface of the glacier, across which rose in deep shadow the mass of the Eckpfeiler and the Péteret arête, its crest brooding under the thin milkiness of the moonlit sky. In front was the great face, incredibly magnificent in the faint light, rising abruptly in dim majesty. All was in darkness, so that vague shape alone could be seen, and the difference between snow and rock scarcely showed in the reflected light from the moon-bathed slopes on the right high above and behind us. We went ever deeper into shadow until distance and size were no more, and we seemed to be penetrating the very essence of a grandeur which knew no measure and had no form. The night was still black, and there was as yet no sign of that slight lifting of the darkness which precedes the dawn.

The traverse of this second couloir or snow-field was easy, and occupied about ten minutes only. Then came another similar slope at the far edge of which was a small snow shoulder where we arrived after a short ascent. Rocks made a re-entrant corner a little farther on, and the ice couloir which descends on the near side of the Sentinelle finds its way down to the glacier in the angle of the corner. We crossed this couloir hurriedly, because it drains a lower ice-cliff which stretches across the flank on our right at the level of the inner end of the snow arête on the old Brenva route and above the Sentinelle bivouac. The going in the rocks now became awkward because of the deepened shadow, and we traversed in them, crossing another ice-filled rock couloir, perhaps one of the several terminations of the great couloir. Finally we reached the rocks at the edge of the steep lower ice-slope near the place from which we had turned aside on 26th July. More ice had been met than on the previous occasion, and another five minutes had been lost on the traverse, so that here, at 4.15, we were a quarter of an hour later than our appointed time.

We immediately set out for the traverse of the broad ice-slope towards the rocks below the Pear. At once we came to the main termination of the great couloir, fortunately spread out in a number of shallow channels instead of a single deep ice run. There was no time to spend on cutting deep steps, and Graven merely nicked the ice in the one or two channels which gave a little trouble. In ten minutes we had crossed this obstacle and then came to another termination of the couloir where the ice run was a little deeper and more awkward, but Graven cut so rapidly that I could only just keep pace in his steps. Next came snow interrupted by ice which we ran across singly whilst safeguarded by the rope, and at last came a final patch of bare and steep ice—the drainage slope below the great ice-cliff on the near side of the Pear. This was about fifty or sixty feet [15 to 18 metres] wide, and Graven ran across it whilst safe-guarded by the rope, so to reach the rocks below the Pear, then I followed and Aufdenblatten followed me, the whole party thus reaching the lower rib. So rapid had been the action that this traverse, perhaps five hundred feet [153 metres] in breadth, had taken twenty-two minutes only in place of the half-hour which had been allowed for it, and we had thus regained eight of our lost minutes. The shadows were about to lift, but the summits scarcely as yet showed the approach of dawn.

At this place we must have been about a thousand feet [305 metres] above the level of the glacier, but still far below the foot of the Pear. The whole flank was extremely steep and exposed, but we had to hurry, because freedom from objective danger was not yet assured. Steep, slabby rocks which were awkward to the crampons now led us up as fast as we could travel. Then followed upward-pointing ribs of rock, which were ill provided with holds. Next came rock and snow mixed. The climbing was not difficult, but a little exhausting because of the rapid pace in the dim light, and it landed us just before 5 a.m. on a little snow point which stood out from the Brenva face at the top of this steep lower part of the rocks. It was here evident that we had reached security, and we therefore halted for twelve minutes to remove our crampons and to sit down. My estimate of our elevation is about 12,630 feet [3,850 metres] but this pretends to be no great accuracy. We had risen about 1,200 feet [365 metres] above the level of Col Moore, and we were probably still more than 250 feet [75 metres] below the foot of the Pear. Dawn was now obviously about to break, and the summits were beginning to show in its forelight.

Leaving again at 5.10 we could now take a more reasonable pace along a fairly narrow arête of snow and then rock which was at first less steep than the rib below but next steepened again as it ascended towards the Pear. The great buttress towered up above us with all its dominance, and, as we were still some distance out from the face, we could just see the upper ice-cliffs peeping over its crest. At 5.20 by my watch, which kept good time, although it may not have been set correctly, these ice-cliffs showed the first faint pink of the rising sun. The rocks were interesting, if not very difficult. Then a 'gendarme' barred the way and was turned on the left by some climbing which led to the neck beyond. Ever steepening, the rocks became slabby and led upwards, whilst the sunlight descended the face to meet us, and dyed the Pear with a dull red which glowed momentarily brighter. We came to the foot of the very steep lower slabs of the Pear and, at the same instant, for the first time cast sharp shadows upon the rocks. We had reached the base of the Pear at the very moment of sunrise.

The Pear buttress is perhaps between eight hundred and nine hundred feet [245 and 275 metres] in height (but that depends upon what you take to be its base), and it is set between the two great lower ice-cliffs which press upon its flanks from either side, the crests of their nearly vertical walls of ice being only a little lower than the top of the buttress itself. The buttress is really shaped like a pear hanging in its natural position, but of course only in relief. The lower rib ends against it at its point of greatest 'girth'. The outer face is therefore very steep and slabby there, but its angle decreases a little higher up, as would that of a real pear, then again to steepen at the pear's neck. But the wonderful North-West face, on which the sun perhaps never shines, is almost sheer in the whole of its great height, and to make a true model you would have to remove a large part of the right half of the pear with one slice of the knife. For even greater completeness, similarly slice the facing side of the pear, but leave the piece in contact after sliding it down a little to the left. There were two places where we thought that we might possibly meet difficulties great enough to stop us—the slabs by which the pear must first be attained, and the 'neck' of the pear higher up, by whatever route we might attack the latter.

We had reached the base of the Pear at about 5.30, the moment of sunrise, and we now went on without pause to tackle the lower slabs, which had looked as if they might possibly prove to be unclimbable at our telescope examination from the Torino hut. They were certainly steep, but not so difficult as we had expected, and we went up in the line of the arête which we had just quitted. Some short but very steep chimneys led to more broken rock in which we encountered two steep slabs, each about ten feet [three metres] high. Above these were snow-covered ledges, which we took as they came, making up and a little towards our left. Thus we reached a larger ledge on the left side of the outer face of the Pear, and there found just enough room for us all to sit down and take our first long rest. The hour was nearly six o'clock, and twenty-six minutes of climbing had served to overcome the first of the passages which had presented doubt. The ascent, unexpectedly easy, had nevertheless been exposed, and also difficult in one or two places. It had landed us at the foot of the more sloping middle part of the outer face of the Pear which, steep as it is, is less steep than are the parts above and below.

Our position was magnificent. The face of the rock fell abruptly from the ledge, for what appeared to be a great distance, into the wide couloir below the left-hand ice-cliff. Far beneath us were the little snow point on which we had halted and the rib of our ascent, whilst far below these again was the surface of the glacier. On our right as we looked out was the very steep flank of the Eckpfeiler with its hanging glacier, still above us. On the other side was a wonderful scene. At our own level, and near at hand, there was a great precipice of red rock, nearly vertical, on the far side of the right-hand ice-cliff. The upper slopes of the old Brenva route were just visible past the edge of this, with Mont Maudit above and beyond them. These all carried their lines down to the right in a splendid pattern. The white silhouette of the old Brenva route fell steeply, then more gradually, to ease at the snow arête (which was a little below our level), and finally to fall very swiftly to Col Moore. Parallel with this, and beyond it, the East arête of Mont Maudit, black and white, fell as steeply until it disappeared behind the outer end of the Brenva snow arête. But Mont Blanc du Tacul caught this sky-line before it fell, and then sent it down on another parallel in the wild and incredible ridge of the Aiguilles du Diable, dark and greatly broken in contrast with the white evenness of the old Brenva route. Beyond that again, the sky-line was captured by the Aiguille Verte, Les Droites, and Les Courtes in a line which fell more gently to the right and parallel with the lower Frontier ridge which stretched along to the Tour Ronde. All these arêtes and ridges and snow profiles were in wonderful contrast, and they lay in sloping lines, each varied from the other, but all proper and apt, so that the whole made a beautiful pattern which was without blemish. The nearer view on that side was also interesting. The Sentinelle, far under our level, clung as it were to the flank below the centre of the Brenva snow arête as seen from this direction, whilst we looked down upon our approach from Col Moore, which appeared to run in an almost straight line towards us from the col, but at a great depth beneath our feet.

We had held two views about the 'neck' of the Pear, or rather, we had kept two strings to our bow in that connection. Far above our present resting-place there is a larger ledge on the outer face of the Pear which seems always to be snow-covered and is a good landmark. The actual ledge could not be distinguished from our low position, but we did see, what we had always suspected, that the rock of the 'neck' rose above the ledge too vertically and unfissured to be climbable. There were therefore two alternatives: either we might ascend to the left by the South-East flank, or to the right by the North-West face. The former had seemed from the Péteret arête in 1932 to offer the easier ascent, but we knew it to be exposed to the danger of ice-fall. My own preference had been for the North-West face, and this we now decided to try. If the description of the Pear given above has been followed, it will be seen that the more broken and less steep part of the outer face ends against, and is extended to the right by, a more clean-cut and vertical part which may be called the 'curtain'. Between one and the other is a shallow and very steep groove or rock couloir, which finally plunges almost vertically to the base of the Pear in what looks like a narrow fissure. The 'curtain' and the North-West face join at a right angle, and the edge of the projecting corner of rock so formed is very sharp, of great height, and nearly vertical, but it is broken at one or two places. We were faced by three problems: Would it be possible to climb the 'curtain' to one of its notches? Would it be possible thence to turn the edge on to the North-West face? If so, could that face be climbed?

We set out again at 6.20 to try our fortune on the 'curtain'. Another shallow rock groove or couloir, now snow-filled, borders the more broken part of the outer face on the left. The ledge on which we had halted was to the left of this again, and we now ascended slabs to the right to gain and cross this couloir. We were then on the more broken rock of the outer face which here, as on all parts of the buttress, was granite of wonderful quality, and very sound. Ledge succeeded ledge, and we went this way and that, but always ascended to the right. The climbing was steep and exposed, but not very difficult, although there were one or two steps more difficult than the others. My recollection is that there was not much choice of route, and the work was always interesting. Rather more than two hundred and fifty feet [75 metres] of such climbing, which Graven called 'nice but not difficult', took us to a point a little below the prominent snow ledge, and at a place where it seemed as if the 'curtain' might be climbed.

Here we traversed the right-hand rock couloir, and Graven was able to climb up and across the steep wall of the 'curtain' to a break or notch on its outer edge which we had seen from below, and for which we had been making. Graven's lead here was a fine and finished piece of climbing. Our position at this point was sensational and very exposed indeed, as it was to continue to be until the Pear was won. It was possible to round the edge of the 'curtain' at this break, and thus we came on to the North-West face. Two of the questions had been answered in our favour. The third remained.

For the first time we could now see the whole of the great ice-cliff on the right (north-west) of the Pear—a mighty thing of vertical ice, soaring above us and descending far below. The North-West face of the Pear we could now see closely for the first time, but its detail was hidden by its own steepness. The splendid rock was split in some places by chimneys, and in others it presented great slabs. Its ledges sloped outwards and were covered with snow, which also filled the crannies in the rock. The true bearing of this face, as closely as I can estimate, is about 20° west of north. I am not certain whether the morning sun in summer may or may not strike across the North-West face for a few minutes after sunrise, but, because the great mass of Mont Blanc rises about two thousand feet [610 metres] higher than the Pear in the North-West and near at hand, it is certain that the sun never shines on the face in the afternoon and evening. The conditions which we met on the North-West face of the Pear—hard ice in the recesses and chimneys and ice and snow on the ledges—are therefore probably always to be expected there.

The rocks of this face now forced us to the right, in an upward direction broken by steps. The rock was slabby, and a ledge would be interrupted by a short rock step, thereafter to continue at the higher level. Some of the climbing was difficult, all of it was exposed, and then, after about a hundred and thirty feet [40 metres]—a little more than a rope's length—of upward movement, we could go no farther on this line. The slabby but fissured face had now to be climbed directly upwards, and this passage of about sixty-five feet [20 metres] proved to be the most difficult on the climb, save only for one short movement a little higher up. Graven, indeed, went so far as to call these slabs 'difficult', but I would myself say 'very difficult'. The exposure there was also considerable. The lower two-thirds, or perhaps three-quarters, of the North-West face are scarcely marked by a single ledge, if by any at all, only the upper part of the face being thus broken. Moreover, the whole face, and more particularly the lower part, is so steep as to appear very nearly vertical from a distance, and of course even more vertical when you are actually on it. At this point there must have been an almost sheer drop of eight hundred feet [245 metres] or perhaps more into the broad ice couloir which drains the right-hand ice-cliff, and that couloir itself descends very swiftly, so merging in the steep lower ice-slope and not easing until it reaches the surface of the glacier perhaps two thousand feet [610 metres] lower down. On the upper part of the North-West face of the Pear that great depth of not far short of three thousand feet [915 metres] appears to be immediately below and without easement or interruption. A falling object would certainly fail to find lodgment until it buried itself in the surface of the glacier beneath.

From the top of the slabs we were now forced up to the left, but for a shorter distance than the first traverse had taken us to the right. This movement presented the same slabby and exposed climbing as before: a ledge up to the left, then directly up, then a ledge to the left again, and so on. In about sixty-five feet [20 metres] we had come towards the edge of the 'curtain' on our left, but not actually to it, and here again a direct upward ascent on slabs had to be made. This passage was about thirty-five feet [10·5 metres] high in all, and it was not in general so difficult as that below, but nevertheless the climbing might be called very difficult, and one short section very nearly beat us.

Our way had been forced so far, and I cannot remember that there was an alternative to any passage, although it is possible that one might have been found had we been put to the test. In any case, the climbing had given the very strong impression that there was no choice of route and that twelve feet [3·5 metres] or less of smooth rock if met anywhere on the way would stop us for good. Towards the upper part of the present slabs an alternative was presented, apparently for the first time. I joined Graven on a slight easement. On either side of a smooth piece of rock there seemed to be a possible line of ascent, barely provided with holds, but each perhaps practicable, if scarcely so. Graven, who told me later that he had been aware of the alternative, chose the line to the right, and was stopped. He said to me (as once before): 'This is the end of the Pear,' and I replied: 'Come down and try on the left,' but he repeated: 'This is the end of the Pear.' So I urged him to try again, and he made a great effort and overcame the difficulty, thus winning the top of the slabs. It puzzled me that Graven had been so convinced that we were stopped for good although there had been at least a chance that the other way might have succeeded, and I asked him about it afterwards. He told me that, as was said above, he was aware of the alternative possibility when he started to go up, and that he heard me suggest it when he was stopped. But he said that the idea that a single unclimbable obstacle could possess no way round had so taken hold of his mind on the previous passages that he could not realize the present possibility and my words seemed meaningless. The absence of choice on these rocks was exactly my own feeling, and this small incident may perhaps illustrate the mental tension produced by that great face.

We now found ledges, interrupted as before, which took us again up to the right. This passage was not so difficult as those below, but considerably longer—perhaps a hundred and sixty to two hundred feet [50 to 60 metres] of upward slant. The way was as exposed as ever, even more exposed at the end, and my recollection is that we had to round a protrusion of rock about sixty-five feet [20 metres] short of the point at which the ledge came to a sudden and dramatic end. The face of the cliff fell sheer from the outer edge of the sloping ledge. From the inside of the ledge, on our left, the rock rose as a smooth and nearly vertical wall. The ledge itself was not suddenly cut off, nor did it dwindle gradually and peter out. It came abruptly to a full stop at the foot of an upright extension of its floor. This was like a shallow pilaster rising from a narrow terrace against the wall of a building, and it entirely blocked the way. There was, indeed, no further continuation of our ledge beyond this obstruction, and the smooth, square-cut, and nearly vertical rock of the pilaster rose until it ended some twenty or thirty feet [6 or 9 metres] higher against the sheer wall of the Pear. Graven nevertheless found sufficient holds in the angle between the main wall and the obstruction to let him win the top of the latter. At that very point, most providentially, the foot of a crack or chimney in the main wall could be entered. This crack rose steeply and brought us out in about thirty-five feet [10·5 metres] on to a small glacis or sloping platform. Here we were nearing the summit of the Pear, and the angle of the North-West face began to ease. Almost vertical rocks still rose on our right, a glance in that direction showing us also that we were well above the level of the top of the great ice-cliff on the right. To the left, looking out from the Brenva face, we could see the slabs of the Pear now sloping at a more reasonable angle. A short snow-filled chimney took us up for about fifteen feet [4·5 metres] to still easier ground, and with that we came into sunlight and freedom again at the top of the Pear buttress. It was now 8.25 a.m., and, in spite of its difficulties, the Pear had occupied but two hours and thirty-five minutes of actual climbing since we had first engaged on its lowest slabs at sunrise. Graven's work had been magnificent.

We went on at once and mounted a snow arête by which we reached near to a small 'gendarme' at 8.35, where we sat down in great happiness. Here, at about, say, 13,780 feet [say, 4,200 metres], we were on the outer edge of the great easement of the Brenva face, which sloped up gently. It is divided into two lateral halves by the continuation of our ridge above the Pear, and the snow collected in these basins discharges as the two great lower ice-cliffs which were now on either hand just below our level. The surface of the left lateral snow-field (that to the south-west) is very much higher than that on the right, and its snow, besides discharging in its great ice-cliff, has also at least two 'overflows' to the right snow-field in the form of ice couloirs which break through our ridge higher up.

The views from this place were tranquil and grand. Looking in, the Péteret arête formed the sky-line on our left, and its flank bordered the great snow-field on that side. To the right was the long and simple gradient of the third snow arête of Route Major, above and beyond which the fine ice-cliffs above the Sentinelle route formed the sky-line. On that side, and farther up, the final buttress of Route Major presented its wonderful outer face of granite and was crowned by the right-hand end of the huge upper ice-cliff. That itself was seen in its fullness to the left of the final buttress, and to the left of it again rose the broken rocks of our present ridge high above the right-hand snow-field, which fell from below the ice-cliff. These rocks ended at the foot of a pillar of red rock which stood up as if to guard what lay above. This pinnacle was the little aiguille which had cast the shadow and so had first pointed the way to this route. It now looked to be a fine needle of rock, its face descending sheer to the top of the rocks above us, its right edge descending almost as steeply to the snow-field on that side.

A well-earned rest had to be brought to its end, and we went on our way at 9 a.m. Almost immediately we came to one of the 'overflows' from the left snow-field to the right, which descended through our rocks as a broad couloir of hard ice. Graven cut across this in three minutes, and then pleasant rocks took us up. These brought us to the foot of a narrow ice couloir which sweeps down from left to right in front of the small aiguille and at the base of its steep face. Up this we went, and so came to a rock couloir behind the aiguille by which we ascended to the neck between it and the Brenva face. From the neck, a short ascent, partly on snow and partly on rock, took us to the summit of the small aiguille, which I was anxious to visit for sentimental reasons. This we reached in rather less than an hour of varied climbing from our last halt. The point itself is fairly well defined, the summit also being sharp, and it stands out well from the face, especially in the views from the direction of the old Brenva route, but it would elsewhere be termed merely a 'gendarme' scarcely worth a visit.

There we built a cairn, and christened the little aiguille with a name of which I had long thought, because, small as it is, this rock had played a significant part in the history of the Brenva face, and for that reason well deserved to be recognized. A name which would signify both achievement and the good fortune by which alone that might come about was close at hand in a forgotten older name of the Aiguille Blanche de Péteret. So I called this little rock the *Aiguille de la Belle Étoile*. If others also use the name it will serve to rescue a beautiful one from oblivion, and will give it a higher habitation than before in its own glacier basin. Although it may be topographically insignificant, this at least may be said of the Aiguille de la Belle Étoile as a climbing objective: there is no way of reaching it save by climbing a route of great exaction. The ascent, moreover, has a reward in store for the climber.

If the visit to this rock had merely been for sentimental reasons, its reward so absorbed me that I forgot to put a record in the small cairn which we had built for the purpose. On the summit of the aiguille, you stand far out from the Brenva face and detached from it by great depth and steepness on all sides save at the narrow arête which descends to the neck. On the far side of that neck, which runs in to the left at 45° to the face, there is another small rock point behind which a second and very broad ice 'overflow' cuts you off from the face. Above that again, a great mass of red and broken rocks leads far up in the line of ascent until it merges in an ice-slope above which is a great ice-cliff. The line of ascent is to lead you up and rather to the left near to the end of the cliff. At a similar angle, but to the right, rises the final buttress of Route Major. We looked straight at the near side of its outer face, one great and almost unfissured mass of granite, fractured at one place, however, where the more broken rock might offer a way up on that face of the buttress. But, immediately above this possible line, the crowning ice-cliff leant forward in the overhanging mass which we had seen on our left when on the top of the final buttress of Route Major ten days before. Beautiful and dramatic as was this sight, it gave an unneeded warning that the outer face of the final buttress should be avoided.

Fine as were these views to left and to right, what lay between was the great reward which the Aiguille de la Belle Étoile gave for its ascent. In mid height (but really lower) we looked across a depth of perhaps three hundred feet [90 metres] into the face of the huge upper ice-cliff, the crest of which must have been at least four hundred feet [120 metres] above our present level. The extensions of this crest in either direction, on to our own upper rocks and on to the final buttress of Route Major respectively, formed the great ice-cliffs at these places, now dwarfed by the face of ice between. That face fell sheer from the level (more or less) of its extensions to left and to right, and it filled the gap between the upper mass of rocks on our present route and the final buttress of Route Major, thus descending vertically through many hundreds of feet. It was perfectly smooth, as if cut by a knife, but it was stratified in a beautiful and regular manner. The top of this huge ice-face actually sags a little at the centre, and the face is delicately marked with ice striations which curve parallel to the line of its upper edge. My estimate of the height of this vertical part of the cliff is about five hundred feet [150 metres]. Below it, and a little below our own level, a curious tongue of ice descended the slope of the easement and looked as if it were pressed out from a hidden part of the ice-cliff like oil paint from a tube. This mass of ice descended steeply, and was probably the remains of avalanches from the upper snow-slopes which fall over the ice-cliff at the sag in its crest. I know of no parallel in the Alps to this great spectacle. The near-facing view of the huge ice-cliff may be obtained only from hereabouts, and in its fullness only from the Aiguille de la Belle Étoile.

The Aiguille de la Belle Étoile may have an elevation of about, say, 14,275 feet [say, 4,350 metres], and we probably still had about 1,300 feet [395 metres] to climb before the summit of Mont Blanc de Courmayeur would be reached. The way was obvious enough—up to the left-hand end of the ice-cliff, then across a wide ice-slope or couloir to the left, then up rocks, which looked to be broken and much like those now immediately above us, and so to the summit. We therefore left the aiguille, descended to the neck, and mounted to the next point, which we found to be a rounded hump. Then there occurred a considerable fall of stones from the summit rocks of Mont Blanc de Courmayeur which we had hoped to ascend. The stones fell down the couloir, but well to our left, and then bounded down the middle of the left-hand snow-field, until they shot over the edge of the ice-cliff on the left of the Pear, there passing out of our view as they fell on to the glacier. We were, therefore, forced to abandon our proposed direct line of ascent up the summit rocks, because these were obviously in an unstable and dangerous state. An alternative and safe way fortunately presented itself. The upper ice-cliff turned in at a right-angled corner from its left end, then to run up the flank on the near side of the ice-slope or broad couloir between it and the parallel summit rocks. In line above this couloir were the terminal séracs, and the whole presented a problem of an exit through séracs very like that on the old Brenva route.

We went on almost immediately, and next crossed the 'overflow' between us and the near rocks—a couloir about eighty feet [25 metres] broad of steep and hard ice. Then came the rocks, which formed a sort of rounded glacis or shallow buttress. This was steep, but the rocks were broken and easy to ascend. Soon we came to a trickle of water from melted snow and paused to make lemonade, because we were thirsty from the heat of the day. The rocks thereafter scattered out in ice, and then the angle of the slope eased a very little and we came not far under the highest of our present rocks in a little less than half an hour's climbing. Here we paused to put on our crampons, and the downward view was amazing. The slight easing of the slope made a kind of near 'sky-line' (or its opposite) below our feet. Looking out to the left down past this, we saw the upper snow arêtes on Route Major which border the great easement on that side. But the easement is considerably steeper and shorter on our present side of the face, and past the 'sky-line' of the near slabs, we looked straight down on to the surface of the Brenva Glacier, there being no object between slabs and glacier save only the summit of the Aiguille de la Belle Étoile, which was outlined as it were against the latter. Another fine sight was also given at this place. We stood fairly near the base of the left extension of the upper ice-cliff, but it formed a slight salient angle to our right looking in, and this hid the great central part of the cliff. That angle, however, towered up as a high and beautiful structure of solid ice which was very white and glistened like highly polished marble.

Now came an interesting piece of ice work. Going on again and walking as much as possible in crampons without cutting steps, we reached the level of the highest of these present rocks and there made a stance. The face of the great ice-cliff was now directly above us, but it ended some distance to our left at the corner from which it turned sharply at a right angle up the steep slope, and a low projection of the ice ran across our path from the foot of the high and cleanly cut corner. Graven, working very quickly, now went along and up towards this projection, nicking the ice where necessary, but also having to cut twenty-two more serious steps. The rope ran out and I had to go forward in the steps before Graven reached the foot of the obstacle in about seventy feet [about 20 metres] of move-ment. There I joined him, and Graven then surmounted the low wall of ice by a delicate piece of work, thereafter passing out of sight but still cutting steps, as was indicated by the sounds and falling fragments of ice. When Graven had reached the limit of sixty feet [18 metres] allowed by the rope, I brought Aufden-blatten up from the place to which he had come forward in turn and then myself went up towards Graven. On surmounting the ice-wall and turning the corner of the main cliff I could then look up the couloir. This was very steep and its near edge, along which we must go, was broken by bulges of ice which protruded from the foot of the upward-running ice-cliff, now close on our right.

Graven stood about forty-five feet [14 metres] higher beneath another projection or bulge, a kind of step in the slope of steep ice which formed the floor of the couloir. I joined him and then he tackled the awkward ascent of the bulge—a mass of hard white ice, glistening and slippery. Then he passed again out of sight and again went on to the sixty-feet limit [18-metre limit] of the rope. Aufdenblatten joined me, and I went for a little way up on the bulge, in order to give Graven the extra rope for which he called. Then I completed the ascent of the bulge, above which ice steps went straight up at the side of the now diminished ice-cliff, but there was no sign of Graven. After I had brought Aufdenblatten to the top of the bulge to give me enough rope, I went up in the steps to reach a place where they rounded a corner of ice, above which there was a break in the ice-cliff on the right. This provided an exit, and I could now see Graven standing above it on a rounded hump of ice at the top of the cliff. Here, amongst the upper séracs, we all came together again. The séracs were splendidly solid, and we stood in the shade of

one for a few minutes, because the day was now almost un-
bearably hot. Then, having threaded a way up and through the
séracs, we came about midday to a place where we could excavate
seats on the side of a mass of ice in a sort of half shade and with
no further obstacle ahead.

All the difficulties of the Via della Pera were now beneath
us, and we rested to enjoy our success and to eat. Hopes which
had often seemed to be unattainable had at last been fulfilled,
and it was a moment for great exultation, but none troubled
me. There was only amazed gladness, so deep that it filled the
throat. I was happy in my company, but longed for absent
friends to be with us, and the memory of those grand companions
who had been less fortunate than I in war came strongly to me.
I wished that they too might have shared this day.

6

The West Buttress
Of Clogwyn Du'r Arddu

F· S. SMYTHE

Frank Smythe, constant partner of Shipton on several Everest expedi-
tions, who also climbed with Graham Brown on the Brenva face of
Mont Blanc, was not pre-eminently a rock climber, which makes this
account of the first ascent of the West Buttress on the biggest and
steepest cliff in England and Wales by a route appropriately known
as 'Longland's' and still graded 'Very Severe', all the more remarkable.
I have included this chapter not only because Frank was a personal
friend with whom I helped to train Commandos in mountain and
snow warfare during the war; but in order to provide the reader with
some idea of the middle years in the history of rock-climbing in Britain.
Frank was a fine writer who could conjure up the atmosphere of a
climb as well as he could describe the beauty of an alpine valley filled
with flowers. Having savoured this climb myself, I can assure you
that those who dared to attempt it in 1921, especially Jack Longland,
the brilliant leader of the enterprise, were very remarkable people.

It was a drowsy day in August 1921 as I trudged up the inter-
minable zigzags of the Gwynant track. Above, a clack of voices,
the popping of bottles, and the pant of a train spoke of Britain's
most vulgar hill-top, Snowdon. I breasted the last rubbish-
strewn slopes and paused for an instant amid the summit hubbub.
The sun warmed; in the west a silver sea streak gleamed over
hazed hill masses; on either hand Crib Goch and Lliwedd
stretched austere arms embracing the sombre waters of Glaslyn

and Llidaw. The clamour triumphed; I bolted down the Llanberis path and turning westwards along the Rangers track
regained quietude. I followed the track and presently turned
right—expectantly. The ground was level for a few yards;
suddenly it fell away; the breeze soughed gently over an edge.
A grey precipice connected the sunny breast of the mountain
with a shadowed hollow where slept a little llyn in a maze of
glacier-born boulders.

An article in the Rucksack Club Journal by Mr H. R. C. Carr
first attracted me to the crags of Clogwyn du'r Arddu. There
are four buttresses—the Far East, the East, the West, and the
Far West. In 1920 only the last named had been climbed, though
Messrs Abrahams had made a short route up the east wall of the
West Buttress. The Far East Buttress is broken and indefinite,
but the East and West Buttresses present the most formidable
rock faces in Wales. The continuity of the East Buttress is broken
by a wide grass ledge running across the buttress at about two-
thirds of its height, the sole break in the smooth sweep of slabs.
The West Buttress is equally unrelenting and looks completely
unassailable. The Far West Buttress slants back at an amenable
angle, and its expanse of rough slabs affords delightful climbing
of a quality comparable to the Idwal Slabs on Glydwr Fawr.
There are several distinct routes, but given a dry warm day
and rubber shoes it is possible to wander almost anywhere. In
such wanderings lies the joy of solitary scrambling, and I was
soon at the foot of the crags. . . .

I found myself gazing up the most impressive slab that I
have seen in Britain. Two hundred and fifty feet high [75 metres],
it slants up to the left in one great sweep, sloping slightly outwards in the same direction. On the right it is bounded by an
overhanging wall; and in the angle thus formed is a narrow cleft
of terrific aspect. The left hand and outer edge of the slab overhangs another and even more formidable slab. The average
width of the slab is about twenty feet [6 metres], and the inclination between seventy and eighty degrees. Up it the eye wandered
fascinatedly while the mind speculated half-dreamily, awed to
passivity. I experienced a feeling that I have not encountered
elsewhere in Britain, the feeling that all mountaineers know
who look for the first time up an unclimbed mountain face, a
gamut of emotion impossible to analyse. But even suppose the
slab to be vanquished, what then? It ended in a small ledge

crowned by a quartz-sprinkled block, and above that the buttress leaned out majestically. We scrambled up the Eastern Terrace and scanned it for a connection with the easier rocks above, but our scanning revealed nothing save a traverse that was only possible to the eye of faith, and the eye of faith is not always the servant of cold reason.

The attempt was made two days later by Longland, Professor T. Graham Brown, Mr C. Wakefield and myself. The weather was not propitious, and ere we reached the foot of the crack a drizzling rain was falling.

There is nothing of ease about the climb; it is difficult at the start, and the difficulty is sustained. First came a narrow chimney. Longland made light of this, and it was evident that he was in good training. At the top of the chimney is a smooth section, to which clung decrepit masses of turf. Now all the best works on mountaineering deplore the use of grass and heather as hand or footholds. Be that as it may, I must confess to deriving great satisfaction from the vegetation decorating the slab, and so I believe did the leader.

Another very steep and exposed piece of work brought Longland to a small stance where it was possible to thread the rope behind a small stone wedged in the crack. Graham Brown was now at the foot of the crack, and Wakefield out of sight below at the corner by the big block. Suddenly—how I do not know—a mass of turf was dislodged and went hurtling down. It harboured in its bosom a large stone which made straight for Graham Brown's head. He had barely time to raise his arm to defend himself when it struck him, fortunately upon the forearm, bruising him severely. Apologies crept down in due course; undoubtedly the climb was in need of 'gardening'.

Longland, having secured himself by the threaded rope, invited me to pass him and try the next section. It was formidable work, how formidable then those who follow will have no conception. One advanced a foot or so at a time digging for holds and removing turf piecemeal; yet the rock beneath was sound, and we were only experiencing what all the early pioneers of British rock-climbing experienced. In a year or so ladies will climb the West Buttress of Clogwyn du'r Arddu and marvel at the difficulties we encountered.

Higher up, the overhanging wall on the right bulged out repulsively. An awkward movement to the left was necessary, and an upward pull on the arms to a small stance. A pebble was wedged in the crack at this point, and after many laborious efforts I managed to thread the rope behind it and thus protect my ascent. The pull was a strenuous one; the overhanging bulge gripped my back lovingly. A haul, a heave, a gasp, a sinuous straining, and it was done. I found myself accommodated in a little corner where dwelt a friendly rock leaf, which would obviously serve both as an excellent belay and a means of descending on a doubled rope.

We became alive to the fact that rain was falling steadily; malicious trickles were beginning to course down the slab and crack; the holds were becoming slimy, and wet holds have a curious knack of dwindling to half the size they appear when dry. There were murmurs from beneath; the tail of the rope, hitherto patient and stoically silent, began to voice its grievances. Longland and I were sheltered and comparatively dry; Graham Brown and Wakefield were wet and cold through inactivity. Retreat was unanimously decided upon; but before retiring Longland climbed past me to a point where he could see something of the route ahead. He returned with the glad news that it would undoubtedly 'go', but that rubber shoes and dry rocks were essential.

As last man down I had no intention of climbing the wet and slippery rocks. I cut off a length of rope, looped it around the rock leaf, threaded the rope through, and after the usual contortions managed to get into a double-roping position and slide off my perch down the airy reaches of the great slab.

Normally there is a certain pleasure to be derived from descending a doubled rope over a steep rock face, but on this occasion the rope was possessed of seven harsh devils, and instead of a dignified progression I proceeded in a series of profane jerks. The wet hemp clung to my breeches and cut cruelly into my thighs, and when I arrived eventually at the grassy recess it was with a feeling of thankfulness that I was still homogeneous flesh and bone and not sawn into two portions.

Thus ended the first round with the West Buttress; but if it had defeated us, it had only done so with the assistance of a perfidious ally—the weather.

Two days later Mr C. A. Elliott, Graham Brown and I returned to the attack, with the intention of exploring from above. The weather was bad, a chill mist enveloped the crags, a biting wind

6

numbed both ambition and fingers, but we gained some valuable knowledge.

The upper portion of the buttress is easy, and we descended with but little trouble to a point some twenty feet [6 metres] above the quartz-crowned ledge at the top of the great slab. From a rocky platform above we gazed down an overhang fifteen feet high [4·5 metres] to the ledge. The rocks are rough and firm, but there seemed small chance of climbing the over-hang, even if the great slab succumbed and the quartz-crowned ledge was attained. The alternative lay in a traverse to the west from the latter round a corner and thence across a steep slab, but it looked a most sensational and tricky piece of work. Yet another alternative was to swing the leader from the end of the ledge down to a shallow groove which appeared feasible. Thence he could ascend and hold the remainder of the party over the traverse from above.

Easter passed and Whitsun came, but the genius of bad weather presided over Clogwyn du'r Arddu. Once more a fierce wind goaded the lynn to fury and rain slashed the crags. Mr R. Ogier Ward, Graham Brown and I, setting out from Beddgelert, explored downwards once more, but got no farther.

On Whit-Monday Graham Brown and Ward unfortunately had to leave. That evening there were rumours of three men having been seen on the West Buttress. On Tuesday a party of us left Pen-y-Pass in two motor-cars, and after sundry adventures, in which a climbing-rope was called upon to haul one car out of a ditch, reached the last cottages of Hafotty Newydd above Llanberis.

Mr G. W. Young accompanied us. The previous day he had ascended the East Peak of Lliwedd by Route II—a great feat and one indicative of his extraordinary arm-power and skill. [He had lost a leg in the war.] We would have given much to have had him with us on Clogwyn du'r Arddu. In addition to Longland were Messrs P. Bicknell and I. Waller, but they were present as spectators and not to accompany us on the climb.

As one approaches Clogwyn du'r Arddu from Llanberis, the crags rise seductively over the desolate upland valley of Arddu. For once the weather was fine and warm. We laboured over the boulder-strewn slopes, perspiring gladly, and scanning the West Buttress for signs of renewed activity. As we gained the well-defined moraine to the north of Llyn Arddu we saw three figures clamber up to the Eastern Terrace to the foot of the climb. There they halted, sat down, and appeared to regard us.

The steep sixty-feet-high [18-metres] wall at the foot of the Eastern Terrace is a wet, loose, turfy, and unpleasant place. Up it Longland proceeded nonchalantly, but when my turn came I must confess that my bad climbing condition, combined with a heavy rucksack, resulted in ignominious failure. Bicknell and I, therefore, scrambled round by the ordinary easy way.

We found Messrs W. Eversden, Pigott, and Morley Wood sitting on the terrace. It was they who had attempted the buttress on the previous day, and they had been very surprised to find the rope sling that we had left behind at Easter. They had got some twenty feet higher than we, and had spent three and a half hours in intensive 'gardening'. They considered the rocks possible above the point they had reached, and had driven in a piton as a belay. But unfortunately the piton had been dislodged, and, unwilling to tackle the section above with no support, they had retreated. Now, and most unselfishly, they advised us to try it, but this we were unwilling to do without them. Lounging on the terrace we expatiated—between mouthfuls of sandwiches—upon the obvious advantages of combining the two parties; it would be happier in every way. They had attempted the buttress and failed, so had we. Clogwyn du'r Arddu could hardly stand the shock from a combined attack by a combination of both defeated armies thirsting for revenge.

We started in the following order—Longland leading, Pigott, myself, Eversden, and Morley Wood as sheet-anchor bringing up the rear.

Conditions were very different from those on our last attempt. The day was warm and the rocks were dry. Longland went ahead in great style, and was soon up to the second stance, with Pigott ensconced above the first awkward slab. Soon came a pull on the rope and a cheery, 'Come on!' indicative of a hoped-for advance on my part.

When Pigott, Morley Wood, and Eversden retire from their professions they will always be able to pick up a comfortable living as landscape gardeners of the severe type. The climb was unrecognizable; where previously one had grasped substantial masses of turf, there was now smooth and uncompromising rock.

'How on earth do you get up this?' I inquired of Pigott, as I scrabbled about on the lower slab above the initial chimney.

'Well, you'll have to use that tuft,' he replied, pointing to a sparse and limp beard of grass hanging over the edge of the slab.

'Glad you've left *something*,' I growled to myself, and, pulling viciously at the beard, sprawled over the edge.

Within twenty minutes Longland passed the stance where our rope-loop of Easter still dangled; Pigott joined him, and Longland progressed to a tiny turfy ledge set some twenty feet [6 metres] higher on the lean face of the slab. Above was the section that had stopped the others on the previous day. There was a long wait; the place would hardly yield softly. I advanced to the rope ring, and Pigott went up to join Longland on his diminutive ledge. Came another long wait. I looked up—two pairs of dissimilar breeches were actively defying gravity above; Eversden, who had joined me, was quietly contemplative; Morley Wood's appreciative grin illumined the depths. Now and again remarks and instructions floated down. 'In there; test it; now stick the rope through; take it gently, and if you get tired come back.' What had actually transpired was that Pigott had thoughtfully carried up two stones in his rucksack; one of them had been cunningly inserted into the crack and a loop of rope cut off and tied to it.

Longland had meanwhile with great difficulty changed into rubber shoes; but even with their aid his lead of the section above was a brilliant piece of climbing. To my mind it is the hardest bit of the ascent, and consists of an overhanging splayed-out chimney from the top of which it is necessary to step far out to the right. It is a long stride, the balance is critical, the handholds mere finger-scrapes, the exposure and the precipice beneath terrific. Only a man at the top of his form, with nerve and skill working in perfect unison, could safely make it. Above was another slab; and if any particular portions of the climb are to be named I respectfully suggest as a suitable title the 'Faith and Friction Slab'. As I vacated the comfortable little hold at its foot I gazed downwards for a moment, and remarked Bicknell and Waller disporting themselves like two tiny pink frogs in the transparent waters of the llyn; whilst on the opposite bank two other pink patches told of Geoffrey Young and his shirt, though at that distance it was impossible to tell which was which.

'Have you got the matches?' inquired Pigott from above. These matches were throughout the climb a constant source of anxiety to Pigott, but on every occasion that we were together we forgot them, only to remember them when we were far apart again. There is, in fact, no portion of the climb which is not associated to my mind with Pigott's craving to smoke and his demands for matches.

The air was breathless and hot; a smooth slate-coloured cloud underhung with coppery billows of cumuli slid lazily over Snowdon; a dusky purple swept down the cwm. Undoubtedly a storm was brewing, and rain was the last thing we wanted on the climb.

Above the 'Faith and Friction Slab' Longland had, in the absence of a good belay, driven in a piton. It was the first that had ever gladdened my eye on a British rock climb; indeed, I understand that at Wastdale Head the hand that can drive a piton into British rock is regarded as capable of pulling a trigger upon a fox. Be that as it may, I have never seen a place, either at home or abroad, that called more for a piton; and I must own to a vast feeling of satisfaction on finding myself attached to it.

Why describe the remainder of the great slab in detail? It is a job for the guide-book writers. No doubt every handhold and foothold will be earmarked and catalogued in the future, because this route is unique so far as I know in Britain. The slab fought to the end—there was never a bit that was not difficult—and finished in a defiant overhang of turf clods. Below this overhang there was a section which was better climbed quickly, for the holds were small, and a man cannot hang indefinitely upon the tips of his fingers. Up it Longland floated with effortless ease and grace. Suddenly there was a shout of joy; he had reached the quartz-crowned ledge; the great slab was vanquished! The shout was taken up by each member of the party, and echoed joyfully around the cwm; our friends by the lake beneath clapped vigorously.

As I followed there came the ominous rumble of moving boulders, and I rebuked Longland and Pigott for thus rudely disturbing the peace of mind of those yet on the Great Slab.

The final section is very difficult, but at the last moment the wandering hand grasps a hold at least as comforting as the

'Thank God' hold on Lliwedd. A stout heave and the body writhes over the top; nothing remains save a few feet of easy work to the quartz-crowned ledge.

The ledge is actually a detached pinnacle separated from its parent cliff by a cleft which is choked with boulders. It was the movement of these that had interrupted my philosophical abstractions on the final section of the Great Slab. The ledge is only a few feet wide, but after the inch-wide holds of the last 250 feet [75 metres] it appeared as a veritable promenade. The situation upon it is amazing; the wall beneath is all but vertical down to the base of the cliff; the face above overhangs. It is the ideal eagle's eyrie of fact or fiction.

Then did Pigott produce his cigarettes, and lo! the matches were forthcoming. A little later we were all united on the ledge, struggling to extricate ourselves from the cobweb of rope that ensnared us.

The fates had been generous; it was not until the ledge was attained that the deluge was released. Had we been caught half-way up the Great Slab our position would have been distinctly unpleasant, especially in view of the leader's rubber shoes, and we should have been forced to double-rope down again—always a tedious business for a large party. But Clogwyn du'r Arddu had dozed that languorous May afternoon, and had awakened too late to preserve its dignity by invoking the aid of the weather. True we were not yet up, but we were within fifteen feet [4·5 metres] of the point we had reached when exploring from above. Certainly those fifteen feet were overhanging; but more than fifteen feet of overhang were required to stop Longland at this stage. Personally I had half-hoped that the previously con-sidered and old-fashioned manoeuvre of 'swinging the leader' from the end of the ledge into the groove up which we had planned to go might be essential. Longland, however, settled the question in arbitrary fashion by clinging up the overhang— the solitary piece of pure gymnastics on the climb—and gaining the platform above. The rest of us were in no particular hurry to follow, and we crouched down out of the rain contentedly smoking, in the pleasant consciousness that Longland was sitting above and getting wet. Finally one by one we strained up the overhang to the familiar ground above.

Some twenty minutes later, and four and a half hours from the foot of the buttress, we were grasping Longland's hand on the summit of the crags and congratulating him upon his magnificent leadership.

It had been a great, a grand climb, and a very happily combined party. Now as we stood on the summit the storm was easing. In the east dim hills peered unsubstantially through a mist veil; overhead the rearguard of fat cumuli shook the last raindrops from their skirts; a steady line of washed blue advanced hard on the cloudy legions of the retreating storm. In the west a bushel of golden sun sovereigns gleamed on the distant sea. Turning, we plunged down into the shadowed cwm.

7

Head-First To Life

HERMANN BUHL

Many climbers are gregarious by nature, enjoying the proximity of their comrades in a crowded mountain hut or camp site, and the demonstration of their skills in competition with others on some much-frequented crag. The brilliant Austrian Hermann Buhl, of impecunious origins, was one of those who, like Noyce, Shipton and Haston, delighted in the company of a few special friends; he often preferred solitude. It was this side of his nature which took Buhl alone to the summit of Nanga Parbat, ninth highest mountain in the world, and back to safety after surviving a night in the open at over 26,000 feet [7,925 metres]; this resounding achievement took place shortly after we had climbed Everest in 1953. When I first met him during a traverse of the famous rock towers of the Drus above Chamonix a few years earlier, Buhl was climbing unroped with his friend Kuno Rainer. He was unroped on the summit ridge of a high Karakoram peak when he fell to his death through a cornice in 1957.

It was Whitsun 1943. I had grown old and fit enough for Service. Field-grey had been fashionable for years, but I had not been old enough. Now I had arrived, though I hadn't yet reached the stage of listening to those deadly little singing birds, the bullets. At the moment my billet was in a particularly beautiful holiday resort in my own native Tirol, St Johann in Tirol, at the foot of the Kaisergebirge—and at the State's expense, too. It was, at that time, the location of the Army Mountain Ambulance School of Training. . . .

What a mixture of stiff discipline and of mountaineering! I found it especially difficult—I, who had always visited my beloved Hills at my own sweet will and caprice—to mould myself to discipline's tight clamp. It was a contradiction in terms: climbers have to be self-reliant, headstrong blockheads or they would come to grief every time the mountains demand initiative or power of decision of them. In the Army you are only allowed to exhibit those fundamentals of the climber's self-imposed training and life's basic aim at times of danger, at the front when attacked by the enemy, and so on. In the early stages of instruction and drill, such characteristics are frowned on; they got me into trouble time and again. What an extraordinary paradox: A Climber-Soldier! I certainly hadn't yet discovered how to fuse the two careers, for at eighteen, I was still more the climber. All the more so, at St Johann in Tirol, where the ridges, faces and teeth of the Wilde Kaiser are more or less on your doorstep.

It was June and I had one day's leave. Waldi and I were together again. Once again we went along the Steinerne Rinne, descending it a little farther than usual. Over our heads the Walls stood sheer, leaving room for only a narrow strip of sky. If you lie down on a boulder there and look to where the two opposing Walls almost touch, you get the feeling that they are both coming crashing down on you. On the right was the Predigstuhl, the West Wall of the central peak still in deep shadow—far too cold for us; so we turned to the sun-drenched Eastern Walls, where rose the precipices of the Fleischbank. The rays of the sun outlined the Plattenwülste even more sharply, till we could recognize that prominent black rift in its exact detail. It was Peter Aschenbrenner and Hans Lucke who found the way up it, many years ago now.

It is not often that a party approaches that part of the Wall; the 'Asche-Luck' hasn't the reputation of being an exactly pleasant climbing-ground. All the same, we wanted to sample it.

'Try a fall with Death,' said Waldi, who likes to face hard facts. In his view one should never underestimate things.

We climbed the first few rope's lengths unassisted. We took no notice of a piton, full of confidence in our own grand form. The next traverse made us quite glad of the rope; but it was not until we reached a roomy pulpit that we got ourselves into full array for Grade VI 'severe' stuff, with twenty-five carabiners, twenty pitons, two 130-feet ropes [40-metres-long] and some rope-slings as our outward accoutrement. An unquenchable upward urge and sheer joy of living were our inner driving force. And somewhere in between was strength, which would be a first essential here. It was the factor which had given me furiously to think on the very first few feet of the gully and had acted as a spur to rouse all my will-power. Extreme difficulties demand extreme bodily and mental concentration. Unassisted climbing was out of the question there; yet there wasn't a piton to be seen on the whole Wall. Could our predecessors have knocked them out on purpose, to rob others who might chance to come that way of the opportunity of using them? We don't know the answer to this day.

We drove piton after piton into the rock, with extreme effort. If I climbed a few feet unassisted, in between, I was so exhausted that I had to knock in another protecting spike immediately. Often I only succeeded at the last possible second. The shaft went ringing into a wrinkle; it had better grip, or—— I soon felt my fingers growing soft as butter, giving way as if they had no bones in them. Quick, in with the carabiner, then pull on the rope—a few more bangs with the hammer: the piton simply had to hold! There I was, hanging from it. I let the hammer slip through my hands and depend from its cord, while I took a short, highly necessary rest, at least till my unfeeling fingers had recovered a little. I wasn't allowed much time for that, because the pull of the rope was making itself unpleasantly felt on my thorax, about which it had become so tightly drawn that immediate release was absolutely essential. 'So it's up to you again, my dear little fingers!'

Another piton driven firmly into the rock, and a sharp upward pull on the rope. I was using every corrugation for my toes. I leaned away, trying to reach up as far as possible, and to place the next spike in another crack at the extreme end of my reach. I placed it perfectly and gave it a well-aimed bang . . . and still it went wrong. The iron shaft flew out and went clinking down into the gulf.

'One piton less, and a "special" at that!' I accused the Fates.

Very carefully I fetched out another, and placed it with extreme care. A lusty bang with the hammer, and the spike went singing into the rift with the old comforting melody, and this time it held. In with the carabiner—hurry now!—and now the rope. But in my haste I hung it in upside down. Never mind!

I was glad to rest after such exertions, even if there wasn't an armchair handy—only a loop of rope round my chest and a couple of tiny projections under my feet. God knows the 'Asche-Luck' of the Fleischbank isn't exactly comfortable.

My legs went doing the 'splits' on the outer edges of the crack, and the climbing became an exercise in acrobatics. My fingers were bleeding, though I hadn't noticed it till I saw the red blotches on the rock.

Another couple of feet gained! Now the carabiners were running out; I had only two left. So I had to retrieve the ones below me each time, which increased the labour and the danger. The sun was getting pretty hot in the meantime. Voices sounded from the Walls all around, but I hardly noticed them. . . . People in the ribbon of a path down there were staring up inquisitively at us. Well might they shake their heads at our choice of a Sunday pastime. Not that I cared—tastes differ.

I wriggled into a crack, forcing my way up. Only a few feet above me, I could see an inviting stance, where I could have a rest; but the rope wouldn't let me move. I cursed and complained. . . . 'Let's have some rope!' . . . There I was, stuck, and couldn't move an inch forward.

Waldemar started agitating the rope; looking down between my legs I could see him manoeuvring it. Still the damned cord ran all over the place; I must have fixed it wrongly somewhere— my own fault. Using the last reserves of strength I could still summon, I tugged at the rope myself; taking it between my teeth, I climbed gingerly up the smooth crack. The slightest slip would mean coming off altogether. At last I reached the stance. Well, stance? Call it a little indentation in the overhang. Those 130 feet [40 metres] had taken me hours.

Then it was Waldemar's turn to come. Almost gloatingly I shouted down: 'Up you come!'

It was particularly difficult for him to follow, especially near the top where I had retrieved all the carabiners. At the start it still went all right, for he was able to pull himself up from piton to piton by the necessary strength of arm, while I hauled the rope in at each movement; but where the carabiners were missing, that method wouldn't do any more. There was only one way; to resort to the technique of the Prusik Knot. He hung the slings on one of the ropes, and I made them fast with the so-called Prusik Knot, which has the peculiar virtue of tightening when any weight is thrown on it, so that it grips the rope, and loosening when the weight is withdrawn, so that you can move it along the rope.

Waldi put his feet into the two slings and went swinging out into space until he was vertically under me in them. Then we were in a position to start the manoeuvre and while he climbed very slowly upwards in the slings, I kept on pulling in the second rope to give him protection. At the end of it, we were both completely exhausted, he from the sheer effort of the climbing, I from continually taking the strain on the rope.

Changing stances was a fearfully chancy business, for there was only room for one man at a time, and then there was all that rope into the bargain. We had to ensure that it didn't get hopelessly 'knitted', to avoid a 'cat's cradle' (to use the trade jargon).

I hung the ironmongery round me once again and started off up another chimney. It narrowed quickly, till its walls were almost touching. The rock pressed heavily downwards and I could only just wedge myself in between by main force. I could see neither up nor down and had to test every hold. I moved carefully forwards by snake-like motions, so as not to go sliding down that open maw again.

When we both stood on a splendid stance in the bottom of a broad chimney above, I said to Waldi: 'I think we've done the worst of it.' But he looked doubtful.

To reinforce my opinion, I told him: 'There's not the slightest doubt it goes straight on up, as Nature dictates.'

I was soon high up on the walls of the chimney. Disgusting country! I shall never learn to like these cold, damp, slimy chimneys; but I was gaining height rapidly, and we could almost see across to the North Summit of the Predigstuhl now. It couldn't be very far to the Ridge now—only another steep bit of rock-wall, overhanging slightly. Only . . .

At a small breach, I spent some time in providing a good, reliable piton. At last I managed to get one in a few inches.

'It'll do in case of emergency,' I thought, and brought my partner along up.

I said to Waldemar: 'How'd you like to fall into that one?— I shouldn't!'—but continued on my way upward. The chimney widened again, till it was too wide to straddle. I climbed up its bottom close to the wall, then traversed out to the right. About sixty feet [18 metres] above my friend's head, I stood on a little stance, panting a bit and examining the way ahead with a critical eye. No, the main difficulties were not finished, after all. . . .

I shouted down to Waldi, warning him to take the firmest possible stance: 'It seems to get difficult again!'

Down in the chimney I could see a little pedestal. It looked reliable enough, and besides, here in the Kaiser, every hold is a sound hold. I straddled in, got my other foot on as well, and stood there quite comfortably on my little plinth, gently massaging my over-worked fingers.

All of a sudden there was nothing under my feet—the block had broken away and was sliding down from under me! I grasped what was happening, instinctively pushing away from the wall with lightning speed. What ensued took seconds to happen. During those seconds I looked out over the edge of life. . . .

Two hundred feet [60 metres] down the chimney, I found myself upright, clinging to the wall, on a tiny shelf. The rope was taut above me—between me and what? That was where Waldemar must be. Everything was so quiet. I hardly dared call up to him. I could only hope the block hadn't hit him. . . .

'Waldi, where are you? Are you all right?'

Down came a voice, choking with joy and amazement: 'Yes! Are *you* alive?'

It was only then that I realized I must have fallen two hundred feet. Two hundred feet, and I was still alive . . . !

Gradually memory began to supply the details—how the block broke away: how I was just able to push off from the rock. Then I was falling: no, rather Waldi seemed to be flying up to meet me . . . past me. Then I felt as if I were floating in thin air—no weight to me any more—rather a pleasant feeling. Finally a dull thump, not in any way sharp or terrifying . . . only as if I had fallen on a sofa or something soft like that. But that wasn't the finish of it. . . . Down I went, from one wall to the other. Suddenly I remembered the piton, of which I had said to Waldi that I shouldn't like to fall down on to it. I felt every bump, but not the slightest pain. Ridiculously enough, I began to think of my new climbing-trousers. I hoped they wouldn't come to any harm from this tumble, they could so easily get torn on the rock! Then my thoughts began to work feverishly. My pocket-knife in my trouser pocket: I mustn't lose that, at all costs. The fall began to seem endlessly long to me. Surely I must be almost down in the ravine at the bottom—only a thousand feet [305 metres] down below, the Rinne! Why didn't the jerk come on the rope? Wildly confused thoughts occupied my mind, but all of them harmless to a degree. Logic, common sense were entirely absent. It never occurred to me that anything serious could happen to me, such as a bad injury; or, if I was to finish up in the ravine, a quick finish to everything. I could feel quite clearly how I was turning over and over—now I was going down head-first. And then at last, the long-awaited jerk. My body was yanked upright, and I was in a normal position again, feet downwards. But I was still falling, falling. . . . Then came a momentary fright: the rope must surely have broken!

Then another jerk . . . my trip had come to its surprising end. By some miracle I was standing quite suddenly on a minute ledge in the wall at the back of the chimney, with the rope as taut as taut above me. I dared not move a muscle, in case I should lose my balance.

At first I felt nothing at all. Only that there was something warm flowing down my forehead. I must have cut my head, for the rock was a little red. But as soon as I tried to grip the wall again, I was aware that my left hand was out of action. Probably I had damaged the bones a bit.

Then Waldemar began to give me assistance with the rope. I climbed up to him and he bandaged my head. Otherwise, except for my left hand, everything seemed in good order. We had to have a good laugh, then, about our incredible luck in such a serious mishap.

Waldemar began to tell me the story, as seen from his watch-tower. . . . I had gone sliding down like an angel—an angel in a hurry, perhaps. Then, head-first, into the chimney, which swallowed me up. A horrid sight, that: unimaginably horrid! Then Waldi had waited for the jerk—the inevitable jerk, which must bring the end. The rope went taut as a fiddle-string, on the verge of breaking, but it held. Then came the moment he had been waiting for, with horror in his heart. The piton would obviously not hold; it didn't, and out it came. The tug of the rope yanked it away from the rock, but the full momentum of my headlong rush had been checked. And then on it went. . . .

Then the rope went taut again; only this time there was no piton between me and him, nothing to act as a brake. It dragged him off and out of the bed of the chimney, to where there was a bigger level spot with blocks piled on it. Desperately he had tried to hold himself and me, but the rope kept on pulling him further out towards the broken edge, towards the abyss below it. . . .

A few more feet—eighteen inches more, now, and the moment would be there when the rope joining the two of us must drag him over the rim. He knew he was for it; the end was staring him in the face . . . at that very instant, at the extreme outer edge of the platform, the drag on the rope suddenly ceased. The rope went loose and Waldi came to rest, there on the uttermost edge. . . . He didn't dare to move or even to shout. Then suddenly, like a deliverance, my voice, from down below.

I do not know even today what Patron Saint stood by us then; but I do know that the whole thing hung on a hair. The more I thought about it afterwards, the more incredible became the whole incident. It wasn't a case of mere luck any more; some kindly Fate took a positive hand that day. Our time had simply not come. God in His Goodness did not want us written-off yet. I had not fallen to my death, but into life itself . . . We promised to celebrate this miraculous second birthday regularly, on its recurrent date, in future.

But as yet it was too early for celebration; we had still to extricate ourselves from the Wall. Waldi still wanted to go on up; I felt it was useless to try. All the same he had a go, but soon agreed that there was no future in it. So down we went, back again, by the long staircase of chimneys. But the huge overhang below gave us plenty to think about.

It simply had to go!

Soon I was beginning to feel the effects of my two-hundred-foot fall. I could feel bruises everywhere, and soon could hardly move my limbs. I lowered myself into the depths of the rope-chair, like a cripple. It was just all right while I was roping down, but when I was on my feet again and had to do a little climbing, it seemed as if I had my legs in splints.

We were now once again in the bottom of the chimney above the huge undercut rift. The sky had meanwhile turned menacingly dark.——— 'Please put it off till we are down in the Steinerne Rinne; just an hour's respite, please—don't let it come down now!' But St Peter was stony-hearted and sent his wet benison in full heavenly measure. . . .

Our 130-foot ropes [40 metres long] hung straight down, dangling well clear of the Wall. Was everything safely anchored? Were the ropes slung properly, so that we could fetch them down after us, when the time came? No question of a retreat, if anything went wrong.

Another look, to make sure, then I went roping down first, in a so-called 'Dülfer Chair': that is, with the rope round my thigh, chest and shoulder, then hanging down loose behind my back.

I grudged every yard of the height we had fought so hard to gain as I went down on the rope, spinning like a teetotum, to the right, to the left, faster and faster. Now it was the Predigstuhl going past, now the overhanging rift was plumb opposite me again. The weight of the rope was unbearable, pulling me fiercely backwards. I could nowhere get a support for my feet on the rock, for the Wall was still some feet away. I felt I couldn't stand it much longer. Supporting one's whole weight with one hand was far too exhausting. So I let myself slide down the rope faster than usual.

That 'misfortunes seldom come singly' is as true in the mountains as anywhere else. So the seam of my anorak hood had to choose that moment to tear and provide more trouble, for now the rope lay against my bare neck and the friction produced unbearable heat and horrible burns; but I was quite helpless and could do nothing about it.

At last I reached the top of the stance under the rift. I had very little rope left, so I tried to start a pendulum-like motion, backwards and forwards, and waited for the moment when my face was towards the Wall, to give a jerk; but I was still a little short.

I swung to the left again like an acrobat on his trapeze. Only here there was no net and I was higher up than the dome of the 'Big Top'.

Again—and I could just get a touch with my feet, while my body pressed heavily on them; at the same instant I had to let go of the rope, to avoid swinging back again, pendulum fashion. This time I managed it.

At last I was standing at the foot of the rift and could shout up to Waldemar to come on down.

'Take care that the rope doesn't stick or get twisted anywhere!'

Then he was wafting down like a spider on its own thread. Opposite me, he swung a bit, till I could get a hold on him and pull him over to my side.

But now came the real moment of tension. Could we yank the rope down? We had to have it for the next *abseil*: without it we could neither rope down nor climb up again. We had taken great care to note the end we had to pull. It was a little difficult, but it went—a little jerkily. We let go of the one end and it disappeared above us; but then, suddenly, it stuck. What was the matter now? It simply wouldn't budge—not an inch.

It must come down! We couldn't stay on the Wall, captives for ever. We used every available ounce of strength on the single end; still it didn't budge—obstinate with the cold and the damp. We swung it about, trying to loosen it, then gave a united 'Heave ho!' That shifted it at last. Very slowly and carefully we began to take it in; faster and faster it ran through our hands, till the joyful moment when it came hurtling through the air like a giant snake. We took a deep breath. We were saved.

One more *abseil* took us down to the Steinerne Rinne. It was quiet down there, not a sound of human life by then. Cold, wet and forbidding, the Walls frowned down upon us. I looked up again at that Chimney! . . . That was the first time I realized how high up we had been. My next thought was: 'And where would we be now if the mountain hadn't been kind beyond words to us?'

Up The Ridge And Down A Crevasse

CHRISTOPHER BRASHER

One of the happy consequences of mountaineering has been its value as a bridge between people from different lands, with different philosophies and backgrounds. I have been very fortunate in taking part in this bridge-building process with Soviet climbers and others; fortunate in that it has enabled me to climb with the Russian, Polish and Czecho-Slovak mountaineers both in their own mountains and in my own country. Before we went to the Soviet Union in 1958 and climbed in the Caucasus, the great Bezingi Wall, which is the subject of this story, had been scaled only once previously by German climbers before the Second World War. It rises with awe-inspiring steepness 7,000 feet [2,133 metres] above the glacier at its base, to an ice ridge which runs for several miles at about 16,000 feet [4,875 metres]. The Bezingi Wall presents the same kind of challenge to mountaineers as the Italian precipices of Mont Blanc.

We woke to find two rough-looking characters sitting outside our tent. They wore high knee-boots and the faded blue, padded jackets that seemed almost a uniform among the Balkarians. Occasionally one of them turned to whistle or throw a stone at a huge flock of sheep that were grazing nearby. They had weather-beaten faces and were unshaven. Yet, there was a curious dignity about them as they sat relaxed, their backs against a boulder, and watched us crawling out of our tents and going about our preparations for the climbs. They were the two Balkarian shepherds who lived with and looked after the village of Bezingi's communal sheep herd, and they had brought us a bucket of fresh milk. They refused any payment for this, but said, if we liked it, they would bring some more the next day.

With the two Balkarians as an interested audience, we packed our rucksacks ready for our four days on the mountain. The basic equipment was a windproof suit, under which one wore either long pants or pyjama trousers and vest, and a woollen shirt. In our rucksacks we packed one or two sweaters, a sleeping-bag or a *pied d'elephant* (literally, 'foot of an elephant', a short sleeping-bag that reaches to your waist), and a *duvet* (a down-filled jacket). We each carried one or two ice-pitons and a small selection of rock-pitons, together with a piton-hammer between each party of two. Cameras, diaries, spare film, spare goggles, anti-sunburn lotion, pieces of string, and some elastoplast completed each man's kit. We filled the rucksacks with food and solid fuel. Between us we carried two Zdarsky tent-sacks—waterproof, nylon bags into which two people could crawl during the night. A rope between two men and a few spare rope-slings completed our equipment.

We set off on a fine, hot afternoon, towards the Misse Kosh—a beautiful meadow between the moraine and the mountain-side. There we stopped for lunch with a friendly group of Russians, including Victor, who were busy fixing a bronze plaque on a large boulder in memory of two Russians who had been killed the year before on Dykh-tau. There were several girls in the group. When I admired the ring of buttercups that one of them had plaited, she immediately took it off and put it on my head. We sat there chatting and eating biscuits and honey with the Russians, reluctant to leave the peaceful meadow and continue our long, hot journey up the glacier. But we had to get to a good bivouac site below our climb before it got dark, so we set off along the hillside while George's party headed down on to the glacier.

Soon we found ourselves quartering up and down the mountainside to avoid the great V-shaped scars cut into the loose, grey, boulder-strewn debris left by the main glacier. It was hot and tiring work, and clear, spring water was becoming rarer and rarer. Far below us on the white, tangled glacier, George, Mike, Derek, and Anatoli had found themselves a smooth pathway between two crevassed areas and were making good time. It was hot work, and even without a shirt the sweat soaked into our rucksacks and poured down our faces. Ahead rose the symmetrical pyramid of Gestola. Our own route on Jangi-tau was just round the corner to the left. And Shkhara was even further out of sight up the glacier.

After two hours of this hard work, when our ankles began to wonder whether they were ever going to get on to level ground again, we came on to the last flat meadow before the glacier turned due east. This was where some of the pre-war German parties had made their base camp. Down the middle of the triangular lawn of grass, which was covered in a torrent of flowers, meandered an icy, clear stream. To plunge one's face into it was as good as drinking a pint of cool Lager.

As we approached the ice-fall, Jangi-tau came into view, with the great Schwarzgruber Rib sweeping down in a long arc to the glacier. It looked awesome. Even from our view-point, where we could see something of its profile, it seemed frighteningly steep. Like a knife edge it soared straight out of the glacier towards the summit of Jangi. I remembered the photograph in an old number of the *Alpine Journal*, with the dotted route of Schwarzgruber's party and the two circles, one a third of the way up and the other just below the summit, where they had had to bivouac. That was in 1935, when the standard of German climbing was the highest in the world, and the Munich 'Tigers' were starting their assault on the north face of the Eiger—the last great problem in the Alps. I felt small and frightened and glad that there were two such experienced climbers in the party as John Hunt and Alan Blackshaw.

But there was no time to stand and stare. We wound our way into the ice-fall, following the Latvians' tracks, and then stepped out on to a shoulder of rock that formed a boundary to the glacier. Three hundred feet [91·5 metres] higher there was a stony valley formed, like the Misse Kosh, between the moraine and the mountainside. Here we found a piece of level ground and dug ourselves a platform for our bivouac.

The sun had set and Jangi towered high above us even though it was nearly a mile away across the glacier. The shadows threw the ice-cliffs of the Bezingi Wall into relief, and we saw what a natural route we had chosen. Everywhere Jangi and the mountains on either side threw down great cataracts of ice towards the glacier. There, in the middle, was our climb, cleaving a passage through the barriers of ice and providing a safe route from all avalanches, to the top of the Bezingi Wall.

We cooked a stew of baked beans and bully beef on Meta-fuel stoves and then, carefully laying out our equipment where it would be easy to find in the darkness, we crawled into our warm sleeping-bags.

I felt the anxiety that is always present before a big enterprise. Ahead of us was a climb that had only been done once before—and then it had taken the Bavarian mountaineers of the best pre-war era three days to get to the top. I lay in my warm bag and looked at the stars so close above—there was no Sputnik racing across the sky tonight to remind us that there were other people in the world. Suddenly the stillness was shattered by the growling roar of an avalanche breaking from the Bezingi Wall. It sounded like the noise of armies waking into battle. And tomorrow we were going to venture up that wall.

I was safe and warm lying in my sleeping-bag on level ground but tomorrow night I might be cramped anywhere on that face with the avalanches thundering on either side. As always before a big climb, it did not seem reasonable. I was afraid of the outcome yet too committed to back out.

'It's two o'clock,' said Alan, shaking me into a drowsy wake-fulness. The cold gripped my hand immediately I took it out of the sleeping-bag. It was deathly still, as if the world was shrouded in ice. There was not a sign of cloud in the sky and the stars seemed to have crept nearer. Even the stream was silent, caught by the cold of the night.

It is better not to think. Every sense tells you to stay warm in your sleeping-bag. I tried to shut my mind off. It is not a complicated process getting up. You are already wearing every-thing except boots and gloves, but they are frozen stiff and the leather must be kneaded until it is supple enough to force your feet inside. We made breakfast, porridge and raisins, and coffee, and stowed everything we could possibly spare beneath a rock. It is surprising how much you can weed from your rucksack when you know you are going to have to carry it on steep ice and difficult rock.

At 3 a.m. we were off, sliding down the moraine to the glacier and heading across this to our rib silhouetted in the moonlight. With our bodies half-awake and our minds still asleep, we walked across the crisp snow, with only the crunch of our boots to disturb the quiet.

The route ahead seemed to divide itself naturally into three parts. At the bottom, the rib threw down a steep buttress of rock on to the glacier. To get on to the rib at the top of this buttress we should have to traverse to the right and make for a snow-slope on its western flank. Once on the crest of the rib there was a section of mixed rock and ice on which the Germans had made their first bivouac. Above that, a perfectly symmetrical snow arête steepened to a snow plateau just below the summit. From this plateau the route traversed left, zigzagging through the ice-fall until it emerged on to the ridge 300 feet [about 90 metres] below the summit of Jangi.

We roped up, John Hunt and Ralph Jones together, Alan and I. Still in darkness, with our head-torches reflecting a feeble light from the ice, we climbed through an ice-fall, across the debris of a recent avalanche, and over a rickety snow-bridge on to the flank of our rib. Alan led up a steep, loose rock-wall and out on to the snow-slope that fell from the crest. At first the going was good. Our crampons bit into the crisp snow so that we could all move together. But the sun was up by now, and the rays were slanting down into our faces and softening the snow surface. We were much fitter than we had been on Pik Kavkaz, and we could maintain good progress up the long slope.

We were no more than a hundred feet [30·5 metres] below the crest of our rib before the snow became really soft and we could feel it balling between the spikes of our crampons. Below there was hard, tough ice. If we were not going to have laboriously to cut steps up the remainder of the slope we should have to move quickly. Alan traversed to the right across thinning snow towards an outcrop of rock. He moved carefully and delicately. The soft snow slithered away and the ice was hard beneath, only allowing the points of the crampons to get a precarious hold. But at last he was on rock. I followed, belayed him around something solid and he climbed up and threw a leg over the top.

We climbed a rock-step and then sat down to a second breakfast. We were now on the crest of the rib and safe from any avalanche danger. It was nine o'clock, and the Germans' first bivouac site was only 800 feet [245 metres] above us. Munching our chocolate we looked around us.

There, like a tiny speck far below, was our bivouac site, crouching beneath the huge rock mass of Dykh-tau with its twin summit blocks plastered in new snow. To the east— our right as we looked out across the glacier—was Shkhara, and somewhere on that steep and icy face was George's party. To the left—the west—we were almost on the same level as the Tsanner Pass which led to the almost mythical valley of Svanetia, down which we hoped to travel to the Black Sea at the end of the expedition. We searched the glacier, but there was no sign of John Neill, Dave Thomas and Eugene Gippen-reiter. A thin cloud hung in the still air, and already the mists were boiling up above the Bezingi Valley.

Ralph Jones and John Hunt took the lead, and we began to feel the rhythm of climbing as we mounted the rocks, moving together. Here, the rocks were more secure except where bands of basalt had been intruded, shattering the rock at its edges. After 600 feet [185 metres] the ridge steepened into a sharp nose, and Ralph turned it on the left up a holdless slab. In crampons it was a delicate move and an excellent lead. Watching the others, I thought it better, with the safety of a top-rope, to try the strenuous chimney above. Inclining along a thin arête and clinging to the rock nose, I stood on the crest of the rib, feeling rather than seeing the dip of a thousand feet [305 metres] behind me. With a long reach, a heave, and a twitch of the rope, I landed on a flat platform beside the others.

Another snow-ridge curving steeply ahead of us, turning the rock-tower that had been the Germans' first bivouac site. We took off our crampons, and John Hunt went into the lead.

It had been hot work, and our water-bottles were already half-empty. Alan and I stayed behind and stuffed snow into them, strapping them to the outside of our rucksacks so that the sun could warm the aluminium and produce water. The snow arête was steepening ahead, and John called back that we should put on our crampons again. When we reached Ralph we saw that John was busily engaged in cutting a staircase up a steep ice traverse with a vertical ice-bulge just above him. He hammered in an ice-piton.

It looked an awesome pitch, with the ice sweeping down

towards black precipices on either side. John had now gained enough height and he was traversing across to the top of the rock-pinnacle, hammering ice-pitons as he went. And then he was silhouetted against the snow with the ice flying from his axe in sparkling crystals. Bringing up the rear, I found it hard enough work to cut the pitons out of the ice. It had been a magnificent and energetic lead by John. It was now only one o'clock and we were past the site of the Germans' first bivouac.

Alan and I took over. Ahead was the second tower, part snow and part rock. It was awkward stuff, with a bulging ice-nose at the finish. Now we could see the third section of the route—the snow arête—and it looked comfortingly short. The Tsanner Pass was below, and we were on even terms with Dykh-tau. At this rate, I thought, we might reach the summit that evening. There was another snow-ridge ahead, but now the sun had done its work and the snow formed great balls under our crampons at every step. There was the oily sheen of ice on our left as Alan led on to the very crest of the ridge. As I drove in my ice-axe and lifted it out again, I could look through the hole, down the sweeping ice-slopes, almost on to the glacier 5,000 feet below [1,525 metres].

We reached a little plateau, a perfect place for a bivouac—but it was only four o'clock and the snow arête looked so short. John Hunt took the lead, over a weak bridge, across a gaping bergschrund, up a steep ice-section, and on to the snow arête. It was at a constant angle of forty-five to fifty degrees, and we plodded on, kicking steps and moving together. Half an hour and we didn't seem to have made any progress.

Alan and I took over. Another half-hour and the arête still climbed ahead of us. We stopped, panting over our ice-axes, beginning to feel the weariness of the long day in our legs. Unnoticed, the clouds had built up around us and there were swirling flurries of snow. Taking turn and turn about, we kicked our way up.

The light was fading and there was still more ahead with the glitter of ice showing through the snow. Alan drove in another ice-piton. Then, at last, we could see an ice-wall ahead and the snow arête abutting on to it, making a simple route to the snow plateau. But we were feeling the height—15,500 feet [4,725 metres]—and we could not hurry.

At last the angle eased. We seemed to be walking on the roof of the world. The slopes fell away on either side. Far below the white ribbon of the glacier shone through a gathering pool of darkness.

I felt a strange, numb weariness. Physically I had been more tired than this, but never before had I experienced such a complete draining of physical and mental energy It was 8 p.m. and we had been moving continuously since 3 a.m.—seventeen hours of climbing over unrelentingly difficult ground. We had had to concentrate at almost every step, for on the sun-softened snow and loose rock it would have been difficult to hold a fall.

We hacked and stamped out a platform in the snow, eight feet by seven, and left a protecting overhang under which we could put our heads. We felt completely dehydrated. During the long day we had only been able to drink the contents of our water-bottles and what we had been able to manufacture by adding snow to them. I lit the stove and filled the pan with snow. Before this had melted the others were asleep.

The wind was blowing in gusts, and flurries of snow were driven on to our platform, putting out the stove. In a state halfway between sleep and consciousness I eventually produced some soup and awoke the others. It was enough for a small mugful each, but it had taken nearly three-quarters of an hour to produce. Alan was hungry and felt he must replace some of his lost energy. He took over the stove to make a stew from our meat bars—a concentrated ration rather like pemmican produced for the Marine Commandos. But before he had finished I was asleep, warm in my magnificent sleeping-bag.

In conditions like this it was a precious object, weighing only just three pounds yet filled with the finest and warmest air-blown down and constructed in such a way that there were no cold spots. It was a New Zealand bag, produced by a man who had done a lot of climbing himself. The same pattern had been used on Everest.

Before leaving England I had taken one of the Everest bags into a shop that prided itself on having equipped numerous mountaineering and polar expeditions. I asked whether they could make a bag to the same pattern. 'Oh, no, we have produced our own pattern since the First World War and it has been very satisfactory.' However their bags only gave half the warmth of my New Zealand one.

The sun woke us at 5 a.m. I still felt lethargic and stiff from the previous day's work. The summit of Jangi was scarcely 1,000 feet [305 metres] above us and our bivouac site was not far below the Germans' second bivouac. We melted some snow for coffee, filled our water-bottles with snow and put them in the sun to warm, and gathered our equipment. Our boots, sodden from their immersion in snow all the previous day, were frozen solid.

It was 8 a.m. before we got away. Immediately we found that the sun had been at work on the snow. It came up to our knees, sometimes our thighs. One could not flog a track through the white pudding for more than fifty yards [45 metres] before handing over to somebody else.

We halted and conferred. With the snow in this condition it was obviously impractical to traverse from the top of Jangi-tau along the ridge to Katuin-tau and descend by another route as we had originally intended.

Throughout our ascent we had said: 'Thank God we haven't got to descend this route.' But now it seemed the only safe way off the mountain. We cached all our bivouac equipment to lighten our loads.

We set off again and traversed to the left and came to a vertical ice-wall. Alan, who was leading, stood on Ralph's shoulders, hammered in a piton, and then secured himself to it. The wall was only twenty feet high [6 metres] but it was vertical and a long and difficult job. An hour later Alan had cut a staircase to the top and we had followed.

Now we had to traverse for 300 yards [275 metres] to the left in order to turn some ice-bulges, and then we would be on the ridge only 200 feet [60 metres] from the summit. But the snow was getting worse. We were ploughing up to our hips through the wet, heavy mass. We crossed a harder patch where an avalanche had cleared the top layers away. Above us an ice-bulge gleamed evilly. It was not a pleasant place to linger. Constantly swopping the lead, we ploughed on.

Ahead there was a large hole where a snow-bridge had collapsed into a crevasse. I was in the lead and I traversed horizontally to get on to firmer ground before crossing the crevasse.

Suddenly I could feel the snow collapsing and I rolled away down the slope as the yawning jaws of the crevasse opened. Picking myself up, I climbed back to the edge of the hole, feeling the ice firm under my crampons. Then, sounding with my ice-axe and staying on the firm lip of the crevasse, I traversed again until the snow-bridge looked more secure.

It was now 11 a.m. and the sun had been on the slope for six hours. I got down on my hands and knees and tried to distribute my weight over as large an area as possible before crawling across the crevasse. Time was getting short and we had to get off this slope before any avalanches started.

John suggested that I should get up and walk, but I could hear the snow settling and groaning beneath me. Once across I dug my ice-axe deep into the soft surface, took the rope in, and then John followed.

Wumph!—there was a large hole where John Hunt had been and the rope was dragging my ice-axe through the soft snow. I put my whole weight on the axe but we were being irresistibly drawn towards the edge of the crevasse.

Suddenly the rope slackened and everything was still.

Alan and Ralph were thirty yards away [27 metres]. I yelled at them to come up and throw a rope down, and we shouted as hard as we could to see if John was all right.

A strange, muffled voice came from the bowels of the mountain. I sat on my ice-axe and took as much pressure as I could on the rope. Ralph and Alan threw a loop from their rope into the hole. Within a minute or two a snow-plastered figure put its head through the hole, and John emerged from the crevasse, looking like a worried Father Christmas.

We had never been happy on this slope and now we had to make a decision as to whether to go on or turn back. There seemed to be more crevasses ahead, and the snow was now very dangerous and so deep and soft that we could not move quickly. The summit of Jangi was only 500 feet [150 metres] above us. We had overcome all the technical difficulties of the climb. Surely it could not be more than two hours before we were on the summit? But we were unanimous that we must turn back.

If we went on now we would only have to wait on the ridge until the evening when the snow would have a chance of compacting again. It was a bitter disappointment. Effectively we had

9

Walking To Everest

WILFRID NOYCE

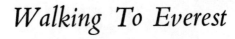

The author of this poem was a very personal friend of mine, with whom I climbed a number of fine routes in Britain and in the Alps, some of them during and others after the last war. We were climbing in the Pamirs with the Russians in 1962 when he was killed after reaching the 21,600 feet summit [6,585 metres] of Pik Garmo. Wilf had climbed brilliantly before the war under the patronage of outstanding men from an older generation, such as Geoffrey Young. I persuaded him, as a war-time officer, to help me train soldiers in North Wales and he played an important part in our success on Everest in 1953; later we had three splendid alpine seasons. Like Dougal Haston, he was something of a dreamer—some would call him 'fey'—whose mind was often away towards some distant peak. I think he never recognized that there were limits even to his exceptional virtuosity: he sometimes failed to see that normal technical precautions were called for, at any rate for lesser mortals like myself, on steep rock and ice, and when traversing a crevassed and snow-covered glacier.

I chose this poem, and the lines quoted in the Prologue to this book, because they provide a glimpse into the mind of this unusual and lovable man.

> Here on the green grass lawn—
> Pine-tree and primula rare—
> Here I would rest and be done,
> By my one self this one,
>   But I do not dare.

Beyond, the hill climbs away
From forest to grass, from grass
White to where snow-tops sway,
Rock-tower cloud-capped grey
   By mists that pass.

Man made to suffer, to stray,
Why must you go beyond?
Fountains your thirst allay,
Torrents their sweetest play
   Here, the still pond.

Sadly the answering heart:
World, you were never mine.
Tiger and snake have art,
Gorged, to sleep out their part
   Of Time's tortured line.

Lost among these comes one
Who cannot once be still.
Sleeping he dreams with moan,
Waking he will not be done
   Until done his will.

Wandering he must know
The first grey peak and the last;
Sunset and polar snow,
Tropic to desert glow,
   Present with past.

And if he suffer for these,
That is his voyage too:
Dim-wrapped in doubts that tease,
Half-lord of doubtful ease,
   He must pass through.

Knowing death is his end,
Death he weighs in his hand.
Where the ice ridges bend,
Where the feat's pride is his friend,
   Straight let him stand.

The Summit: 1953

EDMUND HILLARY

When the time came for me to decide on the summit teams and the various supporting roles for the final assault plan on Everest, one matter was made easy for me. Hillary and Tenzing had shown themselves to be faster-moving and of greater stamina than the rest of us: they made a natural summit pair. I did not include them in the first Assault, because it had a primary purpose of testing the route and the conditions on the South-East Ridge and the arête leading from the South Summit to the top. Hillary and Tenzing undoubtedly benefited from the reconnaissance by Evans and Bourdillon, and from the stores which I was able to leave for them at 27,400 feet [8,350 metres] on the ridge. But the final act in the drama was of their own making.

When writing The Ascent of Everest, *I asked Ed Hillary to tell it in his own words. The two climbers were in their high-altitude tent at 27,800 feet [8,475 metres], which had been pitched on a little sloping snow-shelf on the south flank of the South-East Ridge on 28th May. The support party for this second 'assault', Lowe, Gregory and Ang Nyima, had returned to the South Col.*

It was with a certain feeling of loneliness that we watched our cheerful companions slowly descending the ridge, but we had much to do. We removed our oxygen sets in order to conserve our supplies and set to work with our ice-axes to clear the tiny platform. We scratched off all the snow to reveal a rock slope at an angle of some 30 degrees. The rocks were well frozen in, but by the end of a couple of hours' solid work we had managed to prise loose sufficient stones to level out two strips of ground a yard wide and six feet long, but almost a foot different in levels. Even though not breathing oxygen, we could still work quite hard, but rested every ten minutes or so in order to regain our breath and energy. We pitched our tent on this double level and tied it down as best we could. There were no suitable rocks around which to hitch our tent guys, and the snow was far too soft to hold aluminium tent pegs. We sank several of our oxygen bottles in the soft snow and attached the guys to these as a somewhat unreliable anchor. Then, while Tenzing began heating some soup, I made a tally of our limited oxygen supplies. They were much less than we had hoped. For the Assault we had only one and two-thirds bottles each. It was obvious that if we were to have sufficient endurance we would be unable to use the 4 litres per minute that we had originally planned, but I estimated that if we reduced our supplies to 3 litres per minute we might still have a chance. I prepared the sets and made the necessary adjustments. One thing in our favour was that Evans and Bourdillon had left two bottles of oxygen, still one-third full, some hundreds of feet above our camp. We were relying on this oxygen to get us back to the South Col.

As the sun set we crawled finally into our tent, put on all our warm clothing and wriggled into our sleeping-bags. We drank vast quantities of liquid and had a satisfying meal out of our store of delicacies: sardines on biscuits, tinned apricots, dates and biscuits, and jam and honey. The tinned apricots were a great treat, but it was necessary first to thaw them out of their frozen state over our roaring Primus. In spite of the great height, our breathing was almost normal until a sudden exertion would cause us to pant a little. Tenzing laid his air mattress on the lower shelf half overhanging the steep slope below and calmly settled down to sleep. I made myself as comfortable as possible half sitting and half reclining on the upper shelf with my feet braced on the lower shelf. This position, while not particularly comfortable, had decided advantages. We had been experiencing extremely strong gusts of wind every ten minutes, and whenever I received warning of the approach of such a gust by a shrilling whine high on the ridge above, I could brace my feet and shoulders and assist our meagre anchors to hold the tent steady while it temporarily shook and flapped in a most alarming manner. We had sufficient oxygen for only four hours' sleep at 1 litre per minute. I decided to use this in two periods of two hours, from 9 to 11 p.m. and from 1 to 3 a.m. While wearing the oxygen we dozed and were reasonably comfortable, but as soon as the supply ran out we began to feel cold and miserable. During the night the thermometer read −27° C., but fortunately the wind had dropped almost entirely.

At 4 a.m. it was very still. I opened the tent door and looked far out across the dark and sleeping valleys of Nepal. The icy peaks below us were glowing clearly in the early morning light and Tenzing pointed out the Monastery of Thyangboche, faintly visible on its dominant spur 16,000 feet [4,880 metres] below us. It was an encouraging thought to realize that even at this early hour the Lamas of Thyangboche would be offering up devotions to their Buddhist Gods for our safety and well-being.

We started up our cooker, and in a determined effort to prevent the weaknesses arising from dehydration we drank large quantities of lemon juice and sugar, and followed this with our last tin of sardines on biscuits. I dragged our oxygen sets into the tent, cleaned the ice off them and then completely rechecked and tested them. I had removed my boots, which had become a little wet the day before, and they were now frozen solid. Drastic measures were called for, so I cooked them over the fierce flame of the Primus and despite the very strong smell of burning leather managed to soften them up. Over our down clothing we donned our windproofs and on to our hands we pulled three pairs of gloves—silk, woollen and windproof.

At 6.30 a.m. we crawled out of our tent into the snow, hoisted our 30 lb. of oxygen gear on to our backs, connected up our masks and turned on the valves to bring life-giving oxygen into our lungs. A few good deep breaths and we were ready to go. Still a little worried about my cold feet, I asked Tenzing to move off and he kicked a deep line of steps away from the rock bluff which protected our tent out on to the steep powder snow-slope to the left of the main ridge. The ridge was now all bathed in sunlight and we could see our first objective, the South summit, far above us. Tenzing, moving purposefully, kicked steps in a long traverse back towards the ridge and we

8

reached its crest just where it forms a great distinctive snow bump at about 28,000 feet [8,535 metres]. From here the ridge narrowed to a knife-edge, and as my feet were now warm I took over the lead.

We were moving slowly but steadily and had no need to stop in order to regain our breath, and I felt that we had plenty in reserve. The soft unstable snow made a route on top of the ridge both difficult and dangerous, so I moved a little down on the steep left side where the wind had produced a thin crust which sometimes held my weight but more often than not gave way with a sudden knock that was disastrous to both balance and morale. After several hundred feet of this rather trying ridge, we came to a tiny hollow and found there the two oxygen bottles left on the earlier attempt by Evans and Bourdillon. I scraped the ice off the gauges and was greatly relieved to find that they still contained several hundred litres of oxygen—sufficient to get us down to the South Col if used very sparingly. With the comforting thought of these oxygen bottles behind us, I continued making the trail on up the ridge, which soon steepened and broadened into the very formidable snow face leading up for the last 400 feet [120 metres] to the southern summit. The snow conditions on this face were, we felt, distinctly dangerous, but as no alternative route seemed available, we persisted in our strenuous and uncomfortable efforts to beat a trail up it. We made frequent changes of lead on this very trying section, and on one occasion as I was stamping a trail in the deep snow a section around me gave way and I slipped back through three or four of my steps. I discussed with Tenzing the advisability of going on and he, although admitting that he felt very unhappy about the snow conditions, finished with his familiar phrase 'Just as you wish'. I decided to go on.

It was with some relief that we finally reached some firmer snow higher up, and then chipped steps up the last steep slopes and cramponed on to the South Peak. It was now 9 a.m. We looked with some interest at the virgin ridge ahead. Both Bourdillon and Evans had been depressingly definite about its problems and difficulties and we realized that it could form an almost insuperable barrier. At first glance it was certainly impressive and even rather frightening. On the right, great contorted cornices, overhanging masses of snow and ice, stuck out like twisted fingers over the 10,000-foot [3,050-metre] drop of the Kangshung Face. Any move on to these cornices could only bring disaster. From the cornices the ridge dropped steeply to the left until the snow merged with the great rock face sweeping up from the Western Cwm. Only one encouraging feature was apparent. The steep snow slope between the cornices and the rock precipices seemed to be composed of firm, hard snow. If the snow proved soft and unstable, our chances of getting along the ridge were few indeed. If we could cut a trail of steps along this slope, we could make some progress at least.

We cut a seat for ourselves just below the southern summit and removed our oxygen. Once again I worked out the mental arithmetic that was one of my main preoccupations on the way up and down the mountain. As our first partly full bottle of oxygen was now exhausted, we had only one full bottle left. Eight hundred litres of oxygen at 3 litres per minute? How long could we last? I estimated that this should give us four and a half hours of going. Our apparatus was now much lighter, weighing just over 20 lb., and as I cut steps down off the southern summit I felt a distinct sense of freedom and well-being quite contrary to what I had expected at this great altitude.

As my ice-axe bit into the first steep slope of the ridge, my highest hopes were realized. The snow was crystalline and firm. Two or three rhythmical blows of the ice-axe produced a step large enough even for our oversized High Altitude boots and, the most encouraging feature of all, a firm thrust of the ice-axe would sink it half-way up the shaft, giving a solid and comfortable belay. We moved one at a time. I realized that our margin of safety at this altitude was not great and that we must take every care and precaution. I would cut a 40-foot [12-metre] line of steps, Tenzing belaying me while I worked. Then in turn I would sink my shaft and put a few loops of the rope around it and Tenzing, protected against a breaking step, would move up to me. Then once again as he belayed me I would go on cutting. In a number of places the overhanging ice cornices were very large indeed, and in order to escape them I cut a line of steps down to where the snow met the rocks on the west. It was a great thrill to look straight down this enormous rock face and to see, 8,000 feet [2,440 metres] below us, the tiny tents of Camp IV in the Western Cwm. Scrambling on the rocks and cutting handholds in the snow, we were able to shuffle past these difficult portions.

On one of these occasions I noted that Tenzing, who had been going quite well, had suddenly slowed up considerably and seemed to be breathing with difficulty. The Sherpas had little idea of the workings of an oxygen set and from past experience I immediately suspected his oxygen supply. I noticed that hanging from the exhaust tube of his oxygen mask were icicles, and on closer examination found that this tube, some two inches in diameter, was completely blocked with ice. I was able to clear it out and gave him much-needed relief. On checking my own set I found that the same thing was occurring, though it had not reached the stage to have caused me any discomfort. From then on I kept a much closer check on this problem.

The weather for Everest seemed practically perfect. Insulated as we were in all our down clothing and windproofs, we suffered no discomfort from cold or wind. However, on one occasion I removed my sunglasses to examine more closely a difficult section of the ridge but was very soon blinded by the fine snow driven by the bitter wind and hastily replaced them. I went on cutting steps. To my surprise I was enjoying the climb as much as I had ever enjoyed a fine ridge in my own New Zealand Alps.

After an hour's steady going we reached the foot of the most formidable-looking problem on the ridge—a rock step some 40 feet high [12 metres]. We had known of the existence of this step from aerial photographs and had also seen it through our binoculars from Thyangboche. We realized that at this altitude it might well spell the difference between success and failure. The rock itself, smooth and almost holdless, might have been an interesting Sunday afternoon problem to a group of expert rock climbers in the Lake District, but here it was a barrier beyond our feeble strength to overcome. I could see no way of turning it on the steep rock bluff on the west, but fortunately another possibility of tackling it still remained. On its east side was another great cornice, and running up the full 40 feet of the step was a narrow crack between the cornice and the rock. Leaving Tenzing to belay me as best he could, I jammed my way into this crack, then kicking backwards with my crampons I sank their spikes deep into the frozen snow behind me and levered myself off the ground. Taking advantage of every little rock hold and all the force of knee, shoulder and arms I could muster, I literally cramponed backwards up the crack, with a fervent prayer that the cornice would remain attached to the rock. Despite the considerable effort involved, my progress although slow was steady, and as Tenzing paid out the rope I inched my way upwards until I could finally reach over the top of the rock and drag myself out of the crack on to a wide ledge. For a few moments I lay regaining my breath, and for the first time really felt the fierce determination that nothing now could stop us reaching the top. I took a firm stance on the ledge and signalled to Tenzing to come on up. As I heaved hard on the rope Tenzing wriggled his way up the crack and finally collapsed exhausted at the top like a giant fish when it has just been hauled from the sea after a terrible struggle.

I checked both our oxygen sets and roughly calculated our flow rates. Everything seemed to be going well. Probably owing to the strain imposed on him by the trouble with his oxygen set, Tenzing had been moving rather slowly but he was climbing safely, and this was the major consideration. His only comment on my inquiring of his condition was to smile and wave along the ridge. We were going so well at 3 litres per minute that I was determined now if necessary to cut down our flow rate to 2 litres per minute if the extra endurance was required.

The ridge continued as before. Giant cornices on the right, steep rock slopes on the left. I went on cutting steps on the narrow strip of snow. The ridge curved away to the right and we had no idea where the top was. As I cut around the back of one hump, another higher one would swing into view. Time was passing and the ridge seemed never-ending. In one place, where the angle of the ridge had eased off, I tried cramponing without cutting steps, hoping this would save time, but I quickly realized that our margin of safety on these steep slopes at this altitude was too small, so I went on step-cutting. I was beginning to tire a little now. I had been cutting steps continuously for two hours, and Tenzing, too, was moving very slowly. As I chipped steps around still another corner, I wondered rather dully just how long we could keep it up. Our original zest had now quite gone and it was turning more into a grim struggle. I then realized that the ridge ahead, instead of still monotonously rising, now dropped sharply away, and far below I could see the North Col and the Rongbuk glacier. I looked upwards to see a narrow snow-ridge running up to a snowy summit. A few more whacks of the ice-axe in the firm snow and we stood on top.

My initial feelings were of relief—relief that there were no more steps to cut—no more ridges to traverse and no more humps to tantalize us with hopes of success. I looked at Tenzing, and in spite of the balaclava, goggles and oxygen mask all encrusted with long icicles that concealed his face, there was no disguising his infectious grin of pure delight as he looked all around him. We shook hands and then Tenzing threw his arm around my shoulders and we thumped each other on the back until we were almost breathless. It was 11.30 a.m. The ridge had taken us two and a half hours, but it seemed like a lifetime. I turned off the oxygen and removed my set. I had carried my camera, loaded with colour film, inside my shirt to keep it warm, so I now produced it and got Tenzing to pose on top for me, waving his axe on which was a string of flags—United Nations, British, Nepalese and Indian. Then I turned my attention to the great stretch of country lying below us in every direction.

Meanwhile, Tenzing had made a little hole in the snow and in it he placed various small articles of food—a bar of chocolate, a packet of biscuits and a handful of lollies. Small offerings, indeed, but at least a token gift to the Gods that all devout Buddhists believe have their home on this lofty summit. While we were together on the South Col two days before, Hunt had given me a small crucifix which he had asked me to take to the top. I too made a hole in the snow and placed the crucifix beside Tenzing's gifts.

The Summit: 1975

DOUGAL HASTON AND DOUG SCOTT

Twenty-two and a half years after our British Expedition first climbed Everest, two British climbers reached the top by a much more difficult route, up the 7,000-feet-high [2,135-metres-high] South-West Face. Like the attempts on the mountain by other routes beforehand, several efforts by climbers from different nations to solve this very great mountaineering problem had failed, before the final triumph of Chris Bonington's second Expedition in September, 1975. The feat of Doug Scott and Dougal Haston was, as had been that of Hillary and Tenzing, the culmination of a tremendous team effort; but the bid for the top from above the formidable Rock Band was theirs alone. Like Hermann Buhl and very few others, the climbers endured and survived a night out in a snow cave on their way back. Their own improvised shelter was at 28,700 feet [8,750 metres].

Dougal Haston was later killed in an avalanche, early in 1977.

Doug Scott here takes up the story in the little tent which he and Dougal Haston had pitched in a notch carved out of a snow-ridge, on the brink of the Rock Band, at 27,300 feet [8,320 metres]. The date is September 24, 1975.

DOUG SCOTT   About one in the morning we awoke to a rising wind. It was buffeting the tent, shaking it about and pelting it with spindrift, snow and ice chips.

Because of the intense cold it was essential to put on crampons, harnesses, even the rucksack and oxygen system in the warmth of the tent. Just after 3.30 we emerged to get straight on to the ropes and away to the end. It was a blustery morning, difficult in the dark and miserable in the cold. It was one of those mornings when you keep going because he does and he, no doubt, because you do. By the time we had passed the end of the fixed ropes the sun popped up from behind the South Summit and we awoke to the new day. It was exhilarating to part company with our safety line, for that is after all what fixed ropes are. They facilitate troop movements, but at the same time they do detract from the adventure of the climb. Now at last we were committed and it felt good to be out on our own.

DOUGAL HASTON There's something surrealistic about being alone high on Everest at this hour. No end to the strange beauty of the experience. Alone, enclosed in a mask with the harsh rattle of your breathing echoing in your ears. Already far in the west behind Cho Oyu a few pale strands of the day and ahead and all around a deep midnight blue with the South Summit sharply, whitely, defined in my line of vision and the always pre-dawn wind picking up stray runnels of spindrift and swirling them gently, but not malignantly, around me. Movement was relaxed and easy. Passing by yesterday's tension points only a brief flash of them came into memory. They were stored for future remembrances, but the today mind was geared for more to come. Not geared with any sense of nervousness or foreboding, just happily relaxed, waiting—anticipating. Signs of life on the rope behind indicated that Doug was following apace and I waited at yesterday's abandoned oxygen cylinders as he came up with the sun, almost haloed in silhouette, uncountable peaks as his background. But no saint this.

'All right, youth?' in a flat Nottingham accent.

'Yeah, yourself?'

A nod and the appearance of a camera for sunrise pictures answered this question, so I tied on the rope and started breaking new ground. The entrance to the couloir wasn't particularly good, but there again it was not outstandingly bad by Himalayan standards, merely knee-deep powder snow with the occasional make-you-think hard patch where there was no snow base on the rock. On the last part before entering the couloir proper there was a longish section of this where we just climbed together relying on each other's ability, rope trailing in between, there being no belays to speak of.

The rope length before the rock step changed into beautiful, hard front pointing snow ice but the pleasure suddenly seemed to diminish. Leading, my progress started to get slower. By now the signs were well known. I knew it wasn't me. One just doesn't degenerate so quickly. Oxygen again. It seemed early for a cylinder to run out. Forcing it, I reached a stance beneath the rock step. Rucksack off. Check cylinder gauge first. Still plenty left. That's got to be bad. It must be the system. Doug comes up. We both start investigating. Over an hour we played with it. No avail. Strangely enough I felt quite calm and resigned about everything. I say strangely, because if the system had proved irreparable then our summit chance would have been ruined. There was only a quiet cloud of disappointment creeping over our heads. Doug decided to try extreme unction. 'Let's take it apart piece by piece, kid. There's nothing to lose.' I merely nodded as he started prising apart the jubilee clip which held the tube on to the mouthpiece. At last something positive—a lump of ice was securely blocked in the junction. Carving it out with a knife, we tentatively stuck the two points together again, then shut off the flow so we could register oxygen being used. A couple of hard sucks on the mask—that was it. I could breathe freely again.

Doug started out on the rock step, leaving me contemplating the escape we'd just had. I was still thinking very calmly about it, but could just about start to imagine what my feelings of disgust would have been like down below if we'd been turned back by mechanical failure. Self-failure you have to accept, bitter though it can be. Defeat by bad weather also, but to be turned back by failure of a humanly constructed system would have left a mental scar. But now it was upward thinking again. Idly, but carefully, I watched Doug. He was climbing well. Slowly, relaxed, putting in the odd piton for protection. Only his strange masked and hump-backed appearance gave any indication that he was climbing hard rock at 28,000 feet [8,535 metres].

DS At first I worked my way across from Dougal's stance easily in deep soft snow, but then it steepened and thinned out until it was all a veneer covering the yellow amorphous rock underneath. I went up quite steeply for thirty feet [9 metres], hoping the front points of my crampons were dug well into the sandy rock underneath the snow. I managed to get in three pegs in a cluster, hoping that one of them might hold, should I fall off. However, the next thirty feet were less steep and the snow lay thicker, which was fortunate seeing as I had run out of oxygen. I reached a stance about a hundred feet [30 metres] above Dougal and with heaving lungs I started to anchor off the rope. I pounded in the last of our rock pegs and yelled down to Dougal to come up. Whilst he was prussiking up the rope I took photographs and changed over to my remaining full bottle of oxygen. I left the empty bottle tied on the pegs.

We were now into the South Summit couloir and a way seemed clear to the top of the South-West Face. We led another rope length each and stopped for a chat about the route. Dougal's sporting instincts came to the fore—he fancied a direct gully straight up to the Hillary Step. I wasn't keen on account of the soft snow, so he shrugged his shoulders and continued off towards the South Summit. I don't know whether the direct way would have been any less strenuous, but from now on the route to the South Summit became increasingly difficult.

DH The South-West Face wasn't going to relax its opposition one little bit. That became very evident as I ploughed into the first rope length above the rock step. I had met many bad types of snow conditions in eighteen years of climbing. Chris and I had once been shoulder-deep retreating from a winter attempt on a new line on the North Face of the Grandes Jorasses. The snow in the couloir wasn't that deep, but it seemed much worse to handle. In the Alps we had been retreating, now we were trying to make progress. Progress? The word seemed almost laughable as I moved more and more slowly. A first step and in up to the waist. Attempts to move upward only resulted in a deeper sinking motion. Time for new techniques: steps up, sink in, then start clearing away the slope in front like some breast-stroking snow plough and eventually you pack enough together to be able to move a little further and sink in only to your knees. Two work-loaded rope lengths like this brought us to the choice of going leftwards on the more direct line I had suggested to Doug in an earlier moment of somewhat undisciplined thinking. By now my head was in control again and I scarcely gave it a glance, thinking that at the current rate of progress we'd be lucky to make even the South Summit.

It seemed that conditions would have to improve but they didn't. The slope steepened to sixty degrees and I swung rightwards, heading for a rock step in an attempt to get out of this treadmill of nature. No relief for us. The snow stayed the same, but not only was it steeper, we were now on open wind-blown slopes and there was a hard breakable crust. Classic wind slab avalanche conditions. In some kind of maniacal cold anger I ploughed on. There was no point in stopping for belays. There weren't any possibilities. I had a rhythm, so kept the evil stroking upwards with Doug tight on my heels. Two feet in a hole, I'd bang the slope to shatter the crust, push away the debris, move up, sink in. Thigh. Sweep away. Knees. Gain a metre. Then repeat the process. It was useful having Doug right behind, as sometimes, when it was particularly difficult to make progress, he was able to stick two hands in my back to stop me sliding backwards. Hours were flashing like minutes, but it was still upward gain.

DS I took over the awful work just as it was beginning to ease off. I clambered over some rocks poking out of the snow and noticed that there was a cave between the rocks and the *névé* ice—a good bivvy for later perhaps. Just before the South Summit I rested whilst Dougal came up. I continued round the South Summit rock whilst Dougal got his breath. I was crawling on all fours with the wind blowing up spindrift snow all around. I collapsed into a belay position just below the frontier ridge and took in the rope as Dougal came up my tracks. After a few minutes' rest we both stood up and climbed on to the ridge and there before us was Tibet.

After all those months spent in the Western Cwm over this and two other expeditions now at last we could look out of the Cwm to the world beyond—the rolling brown lands of Tibet in the north and north-east, to Kangchenjunga and just below us Makalu and Chomo Lonzo. Neither of us said much, we just stood there absorbed in the scene.

DH The wind was going round the South Summit like a mad maypole. The Face was finished, successfully climbed, but there was no calm to give much thought to rejoicing. It should have been a moment for elation but wasn't. Certainly we'd climbed the Face but neither of us wanted to stop there. The summit was beckoning.

Often in the Alps it seems fine to complete one's route and not go to the summit, but in the Himalayas it's somewhat different. An expedition is not regarded as being totally successful unless the top is reached. Everything was known to us about the way ahead. This was the South-East ridge, the original Hillary/Tenzing route of 1953. It was reckoned to be mainly snow, without too much technical difficulty. But snow on the ridge similar to the snow in the couloir would provide a greater obstacle to progress than any technical difficulties. There were dilemmas hanging around and question marks on all plans.

My head was considering sitting in the tent sac until sunset or later, then climbing the ridge when it would be, theoretically, frozen hard. Doug saw the logic of this thinking but obviously wasn't too happy about it. No other suggestions were forthcoming from his direction, however, so I got into the tent sac, got the stove going to give our thinking power a boost with some hot water. Doug began scooping a shallow snow cave in the side of the cornice, showing that he hadn't totally rejected the idea. The hot water passing over our raw, damaged throat linings brought our slide into lethargic pessimism to a sharp halt.

Swinging his pack on to his back Doug croaked, 'Look after the rope. I'm going to at least try a rope length to sample conditions. If it's too bad we'll bivouac. If not we carry on as far as possible.'

I couldn't find any fault with this reasoning, so grabbed the rope as he disappeared back into Nepal. The way it was going quickly through my hands augured well. Reaching the end Doug gave a 'come on' signal. Following quickly I realized that there were now summit possibilities in the wind. Conditions were by no means excellent, but relative to those in the couloir they merited the title reasonable. There was no need to say anything as I reached Doug. He just stepped aside, changed the rope around and I continued. Savage, wonderful country. On the left the South-West Face dropped away steeply, to the right wild curving cornices pointed the way to Tibet. Much care was needed but there was a certain elation in our movements. The Hillary Step appeared, unlike any photograph we had seen. No rock step this year, just a break in the continuity of the snow-ridge. Seventy degrees of steepness and eighty feet [25 metres] of length. It was my turn to explore again. Conditions reverted to bad, but by now I'd become so inured to the technique that even the extra ten degrees didn't present too much problem.

DS As I belayed Dougal up the Hillary Step it gradually dawned upon me that we were going to reach the summit of Big E. I took another photograph of Dougal and wound on the film to find that it was finished. I didn't think I had any more film in my rucksack, for I had left film and spare gloves with the bivvy sheet and stove at the South Summit. I took off my oxygen mask and rucksack and put them on the ridge in front of me. I was sat astride it, one leg in Nepal the other in Tibet. I hoped Dougal's steps would hold, for I could think of no other place to put his rope than between my teeth as I rummaged around in my sack. I found a cassette of colour film, that had somehow got left behind several days before. The cold was intense and the brittle film kept breaking off. The wind was strong and blew the snow Dougal was sending down the Nepalese side right back into the air and over into Tibet. I fitted the film into the camera and followed him up. This was the place where Ed Hillary had chimneyed his way up the crevasse between the rock and the ice. Now with all the monsoon snow on the mountain it was well banked up, but with snow the consistency of sugar it looked decidedly difficult.

A wide whaleback ridge ran up the last 300 yards [275 metres]. It was just a matter of trail breaking. Sometimes the crust would hold for a few steps and then suddenly we would be stumbling around as it broke through to our knees. All the way along we were fully aware of the enormous monsoon cornices, overhanging the 10,000-foot [3,050-metres] East Face of Everest. We therefore kept well to the left.

It was whilst trail breaking on this last section that I noticed my mind seemed to be operating in two parts, one external to my head. In my head I referred to the external part somewhere over my left shoulder. I rationalized the situation with it making reference to it about not going too far right in the area of the cornice, and it would urge me to keep well to the left. Whenever I stumbled through the crust it suggested that I slowed down and picked my way through more carefully. In general it seemed to give me confidence and seemed such a natural phenomenon that I hardly gave it a second thought at the time. Dougal took over the trail breaking and headed up the final slope to the top—and a red flag flying there. The snow improved and he slackened his pace to let me come alongside. We then walked up side by side the last few paces to the top, arriving there together.

All the world lay before us. That summit was everything and more that a summit should be. My usually reticent partner became expansive, his face broke out into a broad happy smile and we stood there hugging each other and thumping each other's backs. The implications of reaching the highest mountain in the world surely had some bearing on our feelings, I'm sure they did on mine, but I can't say that it was that strong. I can't say either that I felt any relief that the struggle was over. In fact, in some ways it seemed a shame that it was, for we had been fully programmed and now we had to switch off and go back into reverse. But not yet, for the view was so staggering, the disappearing sun so full of colour that the setting held us in awe. I was absorbed by the brown hills of Tibet. They only looked like hills from our lofty summit. They were really high mountains, some of them 24,000 feet high [7,315 metres], but with hardly any snow to indicate their importance. I could see silver threads of rivers meandering down between them, flowing north and west to bigger rivers which might have included the Tsangpo. Towards the east Kangchenjunga caught the setting sun, although around to the south clouds boiled down in the Nepalese valleys and far down behind a vast front of black cloud was advancing towards us from the plains of India. It flickered lightning ominously. There was no rush though, for it would be a long time coming over Everest—time to pick out the north side route—the Rongphu Glacier, the East Rongphu Glacier and Changtse in between. There was the North Col, and the place Odell was standing when he last saw Mallory and Irvine climbing up. . . . Wonder if they made it? Their route was hidden by the convex slope—no sign of them, edge out a bit further—no nothing. Not with all the monsoon snow, my external mind pointed out.

Over fifty years before Dougal Haston and Doug Scott made their ascent, George Mallory and Andrew Irvine made their final assault on the summit of Everest. On June 8, 1924, Noel Odell was alone at about 26,000 feet [7,925 metres] when a sudden clearing of the atmosphere gave him a glimpse of the summit ridge and the final peak, with two tiny black spots moving up the great rock step. Nine years later, in 1933, an ice axe was discovered under the crest of the North-East Ridge, on the slabs under the first step. Like Doug Scott in 1975, Ed Hillary, too, on gaining the summit in 1953, looked for traces of Mallory and Irvine. He found nothing, but when he and Tenzing had returned to the South Col, Wilfrid Noyce, waiting there, heard him say suddenly, 'Wouldn't Mallory be pleased if he knew about this?' I fancy that Hillary half-hoped that Mallory and Irvine might have been the first, even at the cost of his own unique achievement.

We will never know the fate or fortune of Mallory and Irvine; but I believe, with Wilfrid, that Mallory perceived the prospect of that supreme moment when a human being would first set foot on the summit of the world's highest mountain. as being beyond the realm of mere personal ambition.